Strangers at Sunset

by

Tiffani Lynn

Betrayal to Bliss Book 1

This is a work of fiction. Names, characters, places, and incidents are either the product of the author's imagination or are used fictitiously, and any resemblance to actual persons living or dead, business establishments, events, or locales, is entirely coincidental.

Strangers at Sunset

COPYRIGHT © 2016 by Tiffani Lynn

Contact Information: info@thewildrosepress.com

Cover Art by *Angela Anderson*

The Wild Rose Press, Inc.
PO Box 708
Adams Basin, NY 14410-0708

Visit us at www.thewilderroses.com

Publishing History
First Scarlet Rose Edition, 2016
Print ISBN 978-1-5092-0922-4
Digital ISBN 978-1-5092-0923-1

Published in the United States of America

A beautiful woman, a sexy photographer, a spicy tryst by the sea.

Garrett stops walking and because he's still holding my hand I stop, too. He tugs on my arm a little so my body flattens against his and our lips meet. At first, I'm shocked. My mind tries to comprehend the softness of his lips and the slight tickle of his goatee, so I'm stiff to start out, but it doesn't take me long to warm up. I savor the kiss. It's a connection I've missed. It's smooth, sexy, perfect. He slants his head allowing him to go deeper and my response is immediate as I explore with my tongue.

Just as my libido is waking up from its long nap, he pulls back a little and whispers, "Is this okay?"

Something about that flips my switch. I don't answer him. I just snake my arms around his neck and kiss him this time. It's full of passion and need, almost as if I'm trying to erase this whole year's worth of heartbreak and disappointment.

My hands glide over the contracting muscles of his back in slow motion, savoring every masculine inch of him while he wraps one arm around my waist to hold me tighter. He moves his other hand over my ponytail and tugs the hair tie free. My strands cascade down my back, and he slides his hand up into the hair at my nape helping to control the kiss.

Everyone has tiptoed around me for the last year and stopped treating me like a real person. Most are afraid that they'll hurt me somehow, like there could be more damage done. This is what I need, passion, and an unapologetic, forceful energy.

Dedication

To Teddy—For being the Hero that gave me the real life happily ever after that every woman deserves.

To Kenzie, Tritty & Cass—the selfless support you've all shown me is way beyond your years.
I'll be forever grateful.

I love all four of you so very much!

Author Acknowledgments

They say it takes a village, and after spending the last year writing full time I realize this not only applies to raising children but also to writing a book. This section is where I pay homage to said village.

As always, my family—both immediate and extended—deserves a great deal of credit. I'm the lucky lady who not only has the support of her husband and kids but also her parents, in-laws, aunts, uncles, and cousins. I love and appreciate all you do to make my life as wonderful as it is. Number one thanks goes to my husband though. Teddy, I love that you encourage this crazy dream of mine every step of the way. Thank you!

Also important in everything I do are my friends, both near and far. I couldn't have done this without you. Your help with carpools, sleepovers, phone calls, emails, likes and shares on Facebook, words of encouragement and general belief in my abilities are all priceless. You guys rock! Not to be forgotten are special words of wisdom for my Timberlane Crew— What you find is what you find!

My fellow Merms of Sunshine State Romance Authors, your collective and shared knowledge has helped to make my dream a reality. Dylan Newton, I give you special props for inviting me to join SSRA when I started this journey. This group has been instrumental to my success thus far.

My Snoopy-dancing-partner-in-crime, Judy Swinson, you've made the adventure so much fun. I appreciate you celebrating with me every milestone, both big and small. Thanks for believing in me, cheering for me, sharing your special friendship and making me part of your lovely family.

Author, friend, and mentor, Lexie Post, our long lunches not only inspire me but also provide helpful information and hope for a future in this business. I'll forever be grateful for the time you so graciously give.

This wouldn't be a proper set of acknowledgements without saying a big fat thank you to my Beta Babes. April, Lisa, Judy, Terri, Alison, Barb, Barbie, and Kathy, your insight and eagle-eyes help to create a finished product I'm proud of. Thank you for taking time out of your busy lives to read my work while it's still rough and share your thoughts, ideas and opinions. I love and appreciate you all more than you'll ever know. To April and Lisa, as the first two to read my work, a special note of gratitude goes to you. If either of you would've been less than thrilled I never would have believed this was possible. Love you both!

To Jennifer Glover, my fabulous editor at The Wild Rose Press, I appreciate your patience, reassurance, and guidance during this process. You've made my first experience with a publisher so pleasant. I'm so lucky to work with you!

Prologue

Sirens wail in the distance. The closer they get, the louder they are. *This can't be happening*. I should be waking up in a cold sweat or something, realizing that bad dreams can feel real. Instead, my own heart is racing as I continue chest compressions while the nine-one-one operator tries to keep me calm with a soothing voice. It's almost an out-of-body experience. I know what's going on. Really, I do. My conscious self is sweating profusely and I'm giving CPR to my thirty-two year old husband who collapsed ten minutes ago and stopped breathing. Another part of me, one I didn't know existed, has stepped outside of myself and has become a casual observer to the chaos.

The paramedics finally arrive and take over the chest compressions. A whirlwind of activity ensues. My neighbor, Susan, a woman old enough to be my mother, came over in the middle of everything and is now standing with me as one of the paramedics asks me questions while they load Matt up on the stretcher. I'm trying to make sense of the questions, but just can't seem to do it. I register Susan talking to the short one with the bald head; maybe she's answering the questions. I can't seem to get a grip on reality. The guy who took over chest compressions is still working feverishly. I can see the beads of sweat roll down along his hairline as he continues. The neighbors across the street, Susan, and several paramedics fill the room it seems. My mind is swimming with the warped sound of voices and the rattle of the stretcher as it's lifted and moved out of my front door.

Susan holds my clammy hand tight in her cool, dry one as she tows me to the car. The chilly evening, autumn air nips at my bare arms, but I just can't seem to make myself care. She gets me seated and buckled on the passenger side of the car and rockets off toward the hospital, her foot heavy on the gas pedal. The whole time she's quietly saying things that are meant to reassure me that everything will be all right. I think she knows as well as I do that my husband is already gone. I don't know how I know this, only that I do. I can feel it all the way to the marrow of my bones.

The ER waiting room is filled with the harsh glow of florescent lights and sick people. They are everywhere. Coughs and sniffles ring out around me and the squeals of an angry child barely pierce through the haze that I'm still wrapped in. I know it's an ER in a big city but when I look around, I get flashes of *Night of the Living Dead* running through my head. It's zombie city. Assaulting my nose is the harsh scent of fresh vomit and a hint of body odor in the air.

Susan took my cell phone right after we got here and called both Matt's and my family, but they haven't arrived yet.

We wait for what seems like forever until a man in a white lab coat with a small badge attached to the pocket, that reads *Dr. Charles Childress*, comes out and escorts Susan and me to a small room off to the side.

Dr. Childress is young, probably my age. Not far out of medical school and he looks nervous. His soft, brown eyes dart all around the room and seem to be avoiding contact with mine. I almost want to reassure him that it will be okay, but the reality of the situation slaps me in the face once again and I know without a doubt that it's me that needs the reassurance, the comforting hand. I'm also pretty sure that it's not going to be okay.

We sit down on one side of the table. Susan has her hand on my back and is rubbing slow circles. Dr. Childress, seated across the table, blurts out like he's ripping off a Band-Aid, "We believe that your husband suffered a massive heart attack. We did everything that we could. I'm sorry, he's gone." He lets out a deep relieved breath and turns his gaze to Susan, as I sit trying to process the confirmation of what I already knew in my heart.

"Are you family?" he inquires.

Susan shakes her head and replies, "No, I'm their neighbor. Both Lisa and Matt's family are on their way here."

"In that case, can you stay with her until they arrive? There are certain arrangements that need to be made." He redirects his attention to me and continues, "We can wait for the rest of the family or you can decide now. It's up to you."

I blink, trying to clear the haze that's invading my vision. "I can answer most of your questions now, I think. I know what he wanted. We discussed all of this when we had our wills drawn up."

The doctor nods like he understands. "Would you like to see him one more time, Mrs. Browning? Because of his age, his remains will be sent for autopsy and then can be released to the funeral home. Is there a certain funeral home that you'd like to use?"

"Yes, we will use Murphy's Funeral Home in Amelia. I'd like to see him before he goes."

"Okay, take as much time as you need. Your family is welcome to do the same. Follow me and I'll take you there. I will let the front desk know to be expecting your family. I'm very sorry, Mrs. Browning." His words seem to echo off of the walls as he leads us from the conference room to Matt's room and holds the door open for us.

I step inside the door and my eyes are drawn to his lifeless form. The sheet is pulled up to his shoulders and it's almost looks as if he's sleeping. Eyes closed, face serene. The lack of color to his skin and eerie stillness to his body give him away. I tend to view myself as a strong person, but the massive stone of reality is crushing my chest, leaving me breathless and weighted with grief. *How am I ever going to make it through this?*

Chapter One
Lisa

One Year Later

The phone is trapped between my ear and my shoulder as I rush around my bedroom shoving sandals in my suitcase. I'm talking to my mom, trying to explain why I'm taking a sudden vacation. People have a lot of suggestions on how you should live your life after the death of a spouse and to be honest I'm tired of hearing it all. It's been a little over a year since Matt died and I've heard everything from advice on finances, to advice on ways to start dating again. I'm over it. All of it. I know everyone means well, but I just want some peace.

My mom is having a little hissy fit because she thinks I need to have someone accompany me on this impromptu vacation. Not going to happen. It's a two-fold trip and she doesn't need to know the details yet. The huff of her breath on the other end of the line digs further at my impatience.

"Grab one of your girlfriends or your sister, for God's sake. Don't go alone." Her voice is pleading and strained. "Anything could happen to a woman traveling alone. Besides it will be depressing doing everything alone. You're trying to avoid depressing things, remember?"

Taking a sharp tone, one I never take with my

mother, I say, "Listen, Mom, April has three kids to worry about, and all of my girlfriends have jobs. They can't just up and leave with a moment's notice. Besides, I'm thirty-three years old." I pause and allow a sigh to escape my lips.

"I will be okay. I *need* this. I *need* the quiet. I *need* the peace. Just trust me. I will check in every few days with you or April. I love you, Mom, but I have to go if I want to make this flight."

I can hear the resignation in her voice as she says, "Okay, honey, be safe. Call me when you get there and check in often. You know I worry."

"Yes, Mom, I know you do. I promise to keep that in mind."

"I love you, Lisa." The tenderness of my mother's voice is back. It's the same one she's used on me for years and I melt a little with love for her.

"I love you, too, Mom. I really do. I'm not trying to worry you. I just…need this."

"I know. Call me when you get there. Bye, sweetie."

"Bye, Mom."

I disconnect and toss the phone into my purse. Then I heft my big suitcase off of the bed, and drag it down the stairs and out the door. The cab driver is waiting with the trunk open. He tosses my suitcase in, while I run back to lock my front door. I climb into the cab with one last glance back at my house.

The buzzing of my phone in my purse diverts my eyes from the Cincinnati skyline that is sliding by in the distance. Checking the name on the display, I see that it's my lawyer, Mark. We've spoken more in the last two weeks, than we did in the first few months following the funeral. I answer it and look out the window as we weave in and out of traffic along I-275.

"Hello, Mark. Have you heard anything yet?" I hoped my voice sounded steady.

"No, should hear soon though. Lisa, if the test comes back positive, Jill can fight for half of the estate or possibly more. I think we need to work up an offer to head that off."

I sigh as I respond, "If the test comes back positive, I'll be glad to give up half the estate. I'll sell the house and give her half of that too, but I want it in a trust for the kid. She says she didn't know he was married, but I can't prove that. It's obvious she's after money and I don't mind Matt's money going to his kid, even if I'm pissed as hell at him for this. I *do* mind it going to Jill and her blowing it, or living the high life and the kid never seeing a dime of it. See what you can come up with and we will talk when you get the results."

He's quiet for a minute before he speaks again, "The kid's name is Mariah, by the way. It feels cold to be talking about her like an object, despite the situation. I was thinking the same thing, maybe setting up a trust. I'll start working on that right away. It's possible this is going to get ugly."

"I'm sure it will, but if Jill takes us to court and the judge finds my offer reasonable, then I stand a better chance and it's more likely that the baby…Mariah, will be provided for."

"I've got to say, Lisa, I can't believe you're letting this go without more of a fight."

"If this baby is Matt's, and I believe that she is, then she deserves half of everything that was his. It's only right." I clear my throat hoping to hold off the emotion that's threatening to spill over.

"My heart is broken, crushed, and I'm pissed as hell, but it's not the baby's fault. I'm just not going to give her home-wrecking mother a way to live the high life. I'm sorry I'm so bitter, but it sucked to lose my husband at thirty-two years old, and it fucking blows to find out at almost the same time that he was a serial cheater and I never had a clue. I feel betrayed. I feel like an idiot and I'm so ready for all of this to be over with. Even if the outcome is not what I hope for."

"I understand. If Matt were alive, I'd kick his ass for putting you in this position. I just want what's best for you. We've been friends for a lot of years and I get what you're going through. I just wish I could do more to protect you, to make this easier. You were a good wife. You didn't deserve any of this."

"I know, I agree. Listen, I'm headed out of town for a little bit. Call me when you hear something. Oh yeah, if you run into anyone from mine or Matt's family, please don't say anything. I haven't told anyone but April. I don't want to, unless I have to. Hug Jess for me and we will get together for dinner when I get back." In the back of my mind. I wonder if he's told Jess about any of this. If the roles were reversed, I'd have wanted to tell Matt.

"Okay, have a safe trip. I won't say a word. I'll call you as soon as I hear. Take care, Lisa. Bye." His voice is sincere and reminds me to be thankful that it's a friend handling this for me.

"Thanks for everything, Mark. Bye." I hang up and stuff the phone into my enormous purse. Then I fold my hands in my lap and settle into my memories for the remainder of the ride.

****

Several hours later, I'm stepping off of the plane in sunny Florida. It doesn't matter that it's September, it still feels like it does in July back home. Cincinnati can keep all of the nastiness in my life right now. Give me a beach, some sun, and a drink with one of those little umbrellas in it. I'm hoping that will do the trick. I take note of the choking, humid air and can almost feel the natural curl of my hair frizzing and expanding as I wait for the hotel shuttle to pick me up. The resort is located in a little beach town on the Gulf of Mexico and according to the Internet, it's a *little slice of paradise*. I discovered the hotel while watching a reality show with my niece, about guys who build lavish fish tanks for millionaires and businesses. I think the idea to come here took root while I watched the show.

I climb on to the shuttle and slide into a seat by the window as the rest of the passengers board. I close my eyes and rest my head on the window until we pull out into traffic. The traffic is dense and the industrial buildings dot the landscape for the first few miles, but it doesn't take long for the water to come into view. The sun is high, its rays leaving little sparkles all over the water. It's almost as if someone sprinkled diamonds on the surface. The pelicans fly low in formation before taking turns to dive in the water. I'm already excited and I haven't even set foot in the sand.

Once we unload, I make my way to the check-in counter where the bouncy, young desk clerk slides my room keys and a map of the resort across the counter to me with a huge smile.

"Welcome to Florida, Mrs. Browning. Enjoy your stay."

I thank her and step away from the desk feeling lighter already and follow the map to my room. When I push the door open, happiness in the form of color greets me and I give myself a mental pat on the back for choosing this room. The website called it a *Romance Room* so I debated about booking it, since I'm alone, but after looking at all the other options I knew this was the one for me. It's painted a vibrant yellow and accented with ocean blue and aqua carpets and throw pillows. There are *Guy Harvey* prints on the walls and the furniture is a blonde-colored wood. It looks like a room you'd find at a hotel in the islands. I have a king-sized bed, a huge whirlpool tub, a wall-length mirror, and a balcony that overlooks the beach. Bright, cheery, and comfortable. It's perfect, exactly what I needed.

Since this time last year, it feels like I've only been able to see in black or white. It's almost like the world went dormant when Matt died. This place is refreshing and causes a long overdue smile to cross my lips. Kicking off my shoes, I curl my toes into the plush carpet. I place my suitcase against the wall and head straight for the balcony. There are two plastic white chairs and two white chaise lounges facing the water, so I plop down in one of the chairs, close my eyes, and take a deep, relaxing breath as the sea breeze pushes my hair back over my shoulders.

The rumble of my stomach pulls me back to reality and I realize that I haven't called my mom like I'd promised or eaten since this morning. I groan in frustration as I dig my phone out from the depths of my giant purse. I call my mom to let her know that I'm okay and checked in, and that I'll be texting some, but I'll be relaxing and not to worry.

I stuff my room keycard, some cash, and my driver's license in my little, ivory wristlet and wander down to the tiki bar that sits just off of the beach. It's an open-air bar and grill with the gulf waters as the backdrop. Once I'm perched at a high top table a few feet from the actual bar, I order a frozen strawberry daiquiri and a chef salad. Jimmy Buffet songs are coming from the speakers by the bar, helping to further immerse me in vacation mode. Fried food and ocean air invade my nose and make me almost giddy to think about how far from home I really am.

This last year has been rough. Being a thirty-three year old widow is not something I expected to happen. In fact, of all the scenarios I considered with my life, that was not one that ever even crossed my mind. The other stuff that's popped up in the last six months has been even worse. So, while I'm here I'm going to avoid thinking about any of that, as much as possible, and try to live a little again.

It's late afternoon and it dawns on me that if I finish my drink and shuffle down to the beach I'll be able to catch the sunset. As I'm trying to get the attention of my server, I realize the tiki bar is almost empty. There are only two other people sitting on the other side of the bar. It's right then that a guy, I'm guessing, close to my age, saunters in wearing board shorts, flip flops and sunglasses on his head.

My heart. Stops. Beating.

Suddenly, the air feels heavy and warm, very warm. Like, I-want-to-fan-myself warm.

No shirt, and thank God for that because he has a sexy as hell torso. Skin brown from the sun, and lean, well-defined muscles cover his entire body. Broad shoulders and a masculine chest with a light dusting of dark hair draw my line of sight down further. There is a thin but dark happy trail that starts right under his belly button, bisects the lower portion of his six-pack abs and disappears into his swim trunks. Tearing my gaze away from his lower region, I shift my perusing eyes to his face, specifically, the lush lips surrounded by a dark goatee, then on to his perfect, Greek nose. His dark eyebrows, and short cropped, brown hair match his complexion in the most perfect way. I wish I could stop staring, but I just can't seem to peel my eyes away. It feels obnoxious the way I'm ogling him. *Dear God, please don't let him notice.*

I'm observing this guy as discreetly as possible, while I continue to consume my umbrella drink and wait for the server. No one ever comes to join him and he's not wearing a wedding ring either. His smile is bright as he chats it up with the bartender while drinking his beer. My eyes are laser focused on his lips and throat as he swallows. I can't hear what they're talking about, but I catch the baritone sound of his voice floating on the wind every now and then. His continued smiling during conversation alone would capture my attention even without the body of a Greek god. It's a confident, happy smile with white, straight teeth and the perfect lips for a man. I mean *perfect*.

As the sunset nears, I pay the server and grab my third daiquiri, which he put in a disposable cup for me. Then I wander down to the beach and find a spot on the sand and spend the next half-hour mesmerized by the blue, pink, and purple clouds that streak the horizon as the giant, orange ball sinks into the gulf right before my eyes. It's spectacular, yet peaceful. There is a family a little further down the beach whose kids are still playing in the surf, but otherwise the beach appears to be deserted. My mind drifts to the handsome stranger and I wonder if he's still up at the bar.

Garrett

Most of the time, I love my job. How many people get to travel the world and make a ton of money just by snapping pictures? I know a lot of those people because I'm in that industry, but I come from a blue-collar family so I understand that most people don't get to live like I do.

Sometimes though the assignments are difficult because the subjects are temperamental or an idea for a particular shot just doesn't work out, like now. I've been working on this assignment for three weeks and am still not satisfied with what I have. I thought this one would be easy. I've grown up in Florida and I understand what draws people here. *Enjoy Florida*! is the campaign I'm shooting for so I thought the best place to work on all this was on the beaches. I do plan to head north to the Nature Coast area for some different shots later in the week, but I want the beach to be the focal point. Now, I'm weeks into this project and I still don't have anything close to what I envisioned.

If my muse stays hidden I may have to grab a couple of sexy, young models in skimpy bikinis and head to South Beach to wrap this up. I really don't want anything posed. I've been aiming for natural from the start. You know, real people enjoying the beach here. That's so much more compelling to the average person than bikinis, tans and fake boobs. Although that's all nice to look at, it's been done over and over again. I like my work to stand out. Fresh and original is the hope I have for each project. The fact that I don't go with the expected is what has made me successful to date.

I sling the black bag over my shoulder that holds several different lenses, grip the camera in my palm and leave my room. Stopping for a drink on my way for a sunset picture sounds like a good idea, so I head in that direction. Maxi, the bartender makes me laugh every time I see him and as frustrated as I am right now, I could use that.

As I approach the tiki bar the sound of a familiar Jimmy Buffett tune drifts out of the speakers helping the vacationers get in the right frame of mind. The weathered, faux-thatched roof ruffles in the breeze, but what draws my eye is a mass of long, curly blonde hair. It might be the most beautiful hair I've ever seen. The owner of the hair is turned, looking to the side so I can only see her profile. I can't imagine that the person attached to that mane could be half as gorgeous as her hair.

Her head turns back my way and, so I'm not caught staring, I move the focus of my eyes to the bartender. I round the corner hoping to get a better view without being obvious. I take a stool on the other side of the bar from where I've been sitting all week. Maxi gives me a raised eyebrow and follows my line of sight. He's figured it out. A deep chuckle rumbles next to me as he leans in and says, "She just arrived today. Looks like she's alone and there's no wedding ring." He taps on his ring finger to emphasize the point.

I grin at him and shake my head. Part of what makes him good at his job is that he's observant. I've been in need of female companionship for a couple of weeks now, but nothing has really caught my eye and it's rare that I see the same woman twice. I refuse to get tied down with anyone and if you see the same woman more than once, it's been my experience that they start planning a wedding in their head. One woman even went so far as to merge pictures of our faces on some website to see what our kids were going to look like. The night she told me about that was the last night I ever saw her. I have zero interest in a long-term relationship. Not going to happen. Ever.

When the blonde finally looks up toward the bar area from her high-top table, my jaw drops. She is a knockout. So fucking hot. Delicate facial features, a hint of dimples, high cheekbones, and lashes so long I can see them from here. A long graceful neck leads the eyes to her ample cleavage and if I'm not mistaken, those are God-given, not silicone.

Her thighs are covered by a short sundress. One white sandal rests precariously on the end of the toes on her left foot and her right foot has dropped the other one altogether. I cannot take my eyes off of her. She looks up once and catches me staring so I flash her a smile and turn a little to spark a conversation with Maxi. I'm pretty sure she's watching me, but I refuse to turn and look at her again until I hear her stool squeak with movement. Blondie pays her tab, gives Maxi a finger wave and a small smile, and disappears across the wooden bridge to the beach with a cup in one hand and a wallet or something in the other.

I slam the rest of the amber liquid down my throat and squint when the burn runs its course to my gut. I snatch my black bag up and toss a few bills on the bar.

"I'll be back. I need some sunset pictures," I call to

Maxi as I hurry toward the same bridge she just crossed.

Maxi laughs and I hear in his Jamaican accent, "I bet you need more than that!"

As my feet leave the dock and sink into the warm sand, I'm saying a silent prayer that she's not too far ahead of me. When I locate her, she's not walking down the beach like I expected. She's seated in the sand with her long, sexy legs stretched out in front of her. The hem of her dress is riding high on her thighs exposing more skin, making my dick twitch in my shorts. *Damn.*

She's leaning back on her hands causing her abundant breasts to jut forward. With her eyes trained only on the colorful sunset in front of her the mass of hair is hanging down her back between her shoulder blades. She is breathtaking. Proof that God was listening when I was begging for a muse.

I attach the correct lens to my camera as quickly as I can and start snapping away. I'm waiting for her to notice me, but her eyes never leave that sunset. Her expression changes from content to sad and back to content in the course of time it takes the sun to fully sink below the horizon. At one point she pulls her hair into a thick ponytail, but she never leaves the spot or looks around. I've worked with some of the most beautiful models in the world and none of them holds a candle to this woman. There is absolutely no doubt that I'm in lust.

Lisa

Once the sun lowers beyond the water line, I grab my empty cup and meander along the shoreline, allowing the cool water of the gulf to wash over my feet and ankles. The sky is dark now, but the lights from the hotels and condos that line the beach here leave enough light for me to wander without issue. When I've had enough walking I dust the excess sand off of my feet and slip my sandals back on and cross the bridge back to the tiki bar for another drink.

This time I park myself at the bar. There are a few more people here now. The various tones of voices float across the outdoor space, most of them foreign languages so I have no idea what's being said. Maxi brings me another drink and I sit in silence until he engages me in polite conversation.

He's in his early twenties, Jamaican-born, with the accent to match. He's cute, but young enough that I wonder if he's even old enough to be slinging drinks behind a bar. I tell him I'm from Cincinnati and am here on vacation. We chat for a while until the shirtless guy from earlier returns and chooses a stool a few down from me. He waves at the bartender, holds up a finger, and looks over to give me a polite smile and head nod.

Maxi asks the guy, "Did you get what you needed?"

"No, but I got something better."

I'm trying not to eavesdrop, but I just can't help myself. This guy is sexy as hell and the confident way he holds himself intrigues me. It's not arrogance so much as self-assurance.

"Well, what did you get that could be better than our sunset?" Maxi inquires with a little bit of disbelief in his voice.

"Maxi, the only thing better than a sunset photograph, is a photograph of a beautiful woman enjoying that sunset."

I look over at him wondering where he was taking his photos. There was no one else on the beach, but the one family much further down from me. Our eyes connect and a smile spreads across that handsome face. There is a little twinkle of mischief in his eyes and that's when I realize he's talking about me. Flattered, I can't help myself so I smile back.

I'm wondering how he got pictures of me with the sunset when I didn't see him, but I still haven't said anything, so he takes the reins.

Already in motion he asks, "Do you mind if I sit next to you?"

"Um, no. I mean sure, that would be fine." A giggle follows that and I know I sound like a middle school girl. He plants himself on the stool right next to mine. With a blinding white smile, Maxi glances between us, then turns and drifts toward the other side where other guests are seated.

"I'm Garrett Kline." He holds his hand out for me to shake it, so I put mine out too, and instead of a hearty handshake, he surprises me by lifting my hand to his lips, kissing my fingers with an old school charm very few men our age can pull off. If someone else did that I might find it cheesy, but not the way he did it.

"I'm Lisa Browning." The words come out kind of breathy. It's embarrassing, but who can blame me. This guy is smoking hot and it's obvious that he's flirting with me. It's been a long time since someone flirted with me.

"Are you on vacation, Lisa?"

"Yes, just escaping life for the next week. What about you?"

"Nah, I'm working. It's just a bonus that it happens

18

to be in a place like this. Can I show you what I was working on this afternoon?"

"Sure. I've got nothing else to do." I give him a cheeky grin, with a secret hope that I can remember how to flirt without embarrassing myself.

He turns on the digital camera and pulls up the images he shot earlier. There are some that I'm assuming he took earlier in the day at a different location, then there are the ones he took at sunset. I'm in every single one of them. I should be a little scared that some guy I don't know was taking pictures of me and is now sitting right next to me flirting. Ted Bundy comes to mind, but I sweep that thought away and study the pictures. I wish the screen were bigger so I could get more detail, but even small, what he captured is magnificent. I can't believe I didn't notice him doing all of this. He has several different angles from behind and from both sides. In a couple of them I look sad and in a couple I look content in the moment, which is beautiful. Those are the moments I know I was at peace. I've never had self-esteem issues, but it's been awhile since I looked at myself and saw beautiful. If it wasn't me, I'd be envious of the lady in the pictures.

"Wow. You do amazing work. I can't believe I didn't notice you out there that whole time."

"You seemed pretty engrossed in the view," he states.

"Yeah, some moments are just meant to be savored and that was one of them. If I lived here I don't think I'd ever get tired of that view."

"I agree with you. There are some things that are meant to be enjoyed with the same amount of reverence the first time as the five-hundredth time."

We sit and make small talk for the next hour getting to know each other. His voice seduces me, just with its baritone timber and I relish having the full attention of this sexy man. Thoughts of running my fingertips across the ridges of his abs distract me. I continue to drink and so does he. Maxi comes back and joins in for a short time and before you know it, I'm not feelin' any pain. It doesn't take much with me, but I passed tipsy a while ago. In my head I'm feeling funny and sexy. I hope I'm not acting like an idiot and just don't realize it.

Garrett stands and reaches out a hand to me. "Want to walk on the beach with me?"

If I were thinking clearly, I'd probably say no, just because I don't know this guy. My common sense went out the window with drink number five, so I grasp his hand and say yes. Tingles run all the way up my arm to my spine when we connect and I'm suddenly breathless. This has never happened to me before. When I was a teenager and Matt started to pursue me, I'd get butterflies when he was near me, but never this response.

He pays both of our bills and asks Maxi to watch our stuff for a little bit. His fingers lace with mine as he leads me down to the beach. I'm in a short sundress that buttons up the front and sandals, so I kick off my shoes and leave them by the dock to the beach.

Chapter Two
Lisa

His hand is large and warm around mine and I savor how good this feels after not having this kind of touch for so very long. He leads me down along the water where the waves lap at the sand and never releases my hand. We walk in silence for a while as the water washes over our feet as it breaches the shore each time. Thank God I'm not at the stumbling drunk point, I'm only at the no common sense and sharing too much information point of my drinking.

His brow furrows, as he inquires, "Why are you here alone, Lisa?"

"Honestly? Well, I was widowed a little over a year ago. The last year has been hard, but last week I got some more upsetting news and decided I'd had it. I needed a break from well-meaning friends and family. And from the vultures that want a piece of Matt's estate. And from the pitying looks I get from anyone who has heard the story. I also applied for a job down here and have an interview this week in Orlando."

"You're not seeing anyone?" His surprise is genuine.

"No. Like I said, it's been a hard year."

Garrett stops walking and because he's still holding my hand I stop, too. He tugs on my arm a little so my body flattens against his and our lips meet. At first, I'm shocked. My mind tries to comprehend the softness of his lips and the slight tickle of his goatee, so I'm stiff to start out, but it doesn't take me long to warm up. I savor the kiss. It's a connection I've missed. It's smooth, sexy, perfect. He slants his head allowing him to go deeper and my response is immediate as I explore with my tongue.

Just as my libido is waking up from its long nap, he pulls back a little and whispers, "Is this okay?"

Something about that flips my switch. I don't answer him. I just snake my arms around his neck and kiss him this time. It's full of passion and need, almost as if I'm trying to erase this whole year's worth of heartbreak and disappointment.

My hands glide over the contracting muscles of his back in slow motion, savoring every masculine inch of him while he wraps one arm around my waist to hold me tighter. He moves his other hand over my ponytail and tugs the hair tie free. My strands cascade down my back and he slides his hand up into the hair at my nape helping to control the kiss.

Everyone has tiptoed around me for the last year and stopped treating me like a real person. Most are afraid that they'll hurt me somehow, like there could be more damage done. This is what I need, passion, and an unapologetic, forceful energy.

Just as the kiss reaches a crescendo, where you know that you have to quit or it's going to the next level, a throat clears behind us. Embarrassed, I jump back a little. Garrett chuckles and grabs my hand to steady me. I look behind us to find an older couple giving us the evil eye. I give a repentant shrug as he pulls me aside so they can pass.

My heart is hammering in my chest still which I'm certain has more to do with the kiss than just getting caught making out like a couple of teenagers. Instead of kissing me again, he lets go of my hand and pushes loose tendrils of my hair away from my face. His thumb runs across my cheek, the movement so light it sends shivers all the way down my body. The fingers continue their gentle survey of my skin moving along my neck, over my bare shoulders and down my arms. I close my eyes immersing myself in his tenderness and the heat he's building between us. When his hands come back to cup my jaw on both sides he stares right into my eyes, seeming to burn right through me he whispers, "You are so incredibly beautiful."

I've been told this before, but there is something about the way he's looking at me, like he's cataloging everything he likes from top to bottom not missing even the most miniscule thing. That kind of attention from this particular man is melting me. His face moves closer, his lips so close I feel his breath feather against mine. His subtle moves have my body burning hot, from the inside out.

I can't hold back any longer, so I close that tiny distance between us. Pressing my lips to his, I lick the seam, begging entrance and he doesn't hesitate, opening for me. He lets me take what I want, what my body says I need. My arms wrap around his shoulders, my fingers trail along the trimmed hair at his nape. It has a slight prickly texture, but was so soft. He releases a soft growl and our kiss grows hungry again like we are both starving and we've found the feast. His hands shift from my back to run up my sides, over my rib cage until they reach my breasts. He cups his hands under the fleshy weight, around the nipple, but not touching it. My tight peaks are dying for his attention but he continues to tease me, grazing the edges, never making direct contact.

He's drawing this out, making me wetter with each brush of his lips and touch of his hands. His lips break from mine and trail down my neck nipping and licking, creating little stings that enhance the pleasure of his mouth on my skin. His fingers work the buttons of my dress and they slide inside and over the lace of my bra. A whimper escapes from the back of my throat and my head tilts backwards. I'm lost to the wet heat of his mouth as it encloses around my covered peak. He's teasing first one side with lips and tongue and even a little teeth before he moves to the other side.

I must be holding my breath because I'm feeling a little dizzy when he stops abruptly. He lifts his head and holds me tight against his chest. I can't quite figure out what's going on so I stand still waiting for…I don't know what. *Is he changing his mind? Does he want to stop? Dear God, please don't let him stop.* My body is like an inferno. He can't leave me like this.

Leaning down to whisper in my ear he says, "Jogger. Just hold tight."

My lust-addled brain wonders what that means. I can't quite figure it out until I hear the telltale cadence of a jogger's footsteps approaching and then receding.

"Where are all these people coming from?" he murmurs right before he takes up where he left off. Tired of holding back, I become more brazen in my exploration of his body by running my palm down his tight abs. They contract under my fingers. I continue following the happy trail and graze my fingers over his straining erection. He groans and I smile against his lips. I grip him the best that I can through the shorts and begin to caress him up and down keeping my pace slow. Acting on instinct, his hips flex against my hand and it seems that his control snaps.

Garrett's movements become a little jerky before he grasps my wrist, removing it. Then he maneuvers me a little further up into the sand, away from the surf. Despite this raging inferno building between us, he still seems to have enough thought to pull me down to the ground as careful as possible. However, as soon as my back makes contact with the grainy sand, he's on me. My senses are fogged by alcohol and lust in its most primitive form.

I can feel the coarseness of his goatee as he licks and sucks a gentle line down my throat. I'm on my back next to him while his hands caress the outside of my thighs and under my dress to the curve of my behind. He squeezes the flesh with his big, strong hands. He runs his hand back down my thigh and hitches it up over his leg, changing direction his hand travels on the inside of my thigh to my wet center. His fingers glide along the damp seam of my panties with just enough pressure to make me whimper.

As his fingers move my panties out of the way to stroke the soft flesh, his lips suck and lick my earlobe causing my body to shiver. When I open my clenched eyes a million little stars twinkle in the heavens above us. It's like a scene in a movie. In a brief moment of lucidity, I wonder if we are giving anyone a show until I feel one of his thick fingers enter me, and then all rational thought leaves me again. The burning feeling is back and it's spread from head to toe.

My mind has now stopped working and my body has taken over. Instinct and lust are running the show like a tightly wound Broadway stage director. I push my hand under the waistband of his board shorts seeking his rock hard flesh. I grip his warm shaft in my fist realizing that my hand can't fit all the way around it. I pump him with the smoothest strokes my fevered hands will allow. He lets out a soft groan and slides a second finger into me while circling my clit in the perfect rhythm with his thumb.

His kisses become harder and more fervent as I continue to work him. At the same time, he's building my orgasm to a fevered pitch, almost the breaking point, I'm ready to go over the edge when he pulls his hand away and pushes my dress higher. I almost cry at the loss. Needing, wanting, dying to finish. My mind tries to peel its way out of the lusty fog to recognize that I'm on a public beach having one of the hottest moments of my life where anyone can see us, but it's not working.

Halting my thoughts once again he crawls in between my legs, eyes connected with mine and I'm so glad there is enough light for me to watch his face. He unbuttons more of my dress exposing my straining breasts against the red lace bra. With a gentle touch, he trails his fingers over the scalloped edges along the swell of my heaving mounds and pulls the fabric down under my right breast, trussing it up. His tongue peeks out and swipes the beaded tip. Restless, I mewl for more. His shaking fingers tug the lace on the other side exposing that breast too. Instead of a swipe of the tongue this time, his lips close over my nipple and he sucks hard. I cry out begging him for more.

His impatience must be growing along with my own because instead of divesting me of the bra or going back for more he lowers himself and aligns his clothed hardness with my exposed softness. His elbows are on both sides of my head as he grinds against me hitting the necessary spot. I'm feeling needy and out of control, wanting this so bad that I yank on his shorts trying to get them down. He sits back on his heels breathless and asks, "Are you sure? You want this?"

I know I should take a moment to think about this. I'm a grown woman on a public beach for goodness sake, but I run my eyes from his down the length of his body admiring every exposed inch and realize I don't care about the consequences. I don't care if we get caught. I just want a piece of the sexy photographer crouched in front of me. His eyes study me like a predator does his prey. I throw caution to the wind hoping to silence my inner dialogue and say, "Yes. Yes. Please." I know I sound desperate. I'm almost begging, but I just don't give a crap right now. I haven't felt this good, this awake, or this alive in a long, long time.

He hooks his hands in the sides of my panties and rips them off as easy as if they were made of paper, tossing them aside. I let out a surprised squeak realizing that Matt never did that. He was never so overrun with lust for me that he'd rather rip my panties off, than take the time to pull them down my legs.

Garrett glances around like he's just remembered that there could be people nearby, raises his body up, and drops his shorts to the ground. He is outlined by the moonlight giving the moment a dream-like quality I know I'll never forget.

Before I can think, or even breathe, he's back down

over me, his knees spread wide as he enters my channel with a strong thrust. I arch my back in ecstasy and wrap my legs around his waist. His groan vibrates through me and I lean up to suck the soft flesh of his ear lobe between my lips and run my tongue down his neck. My hips rise to meet him as he pumps into me over and over and over again. I can feel the swell of the climax that is sure to consume me building quicker and more powerful than I knew was possible. I'm fighting it, praying for it to last longer, but the pressure and excitement consume me and I come apart under him. There is a burst of light behind my eyes as my body is writhing out of control, clenching him from within as I scream out his name.

"Garrett! Oh God, Garrett!"

My nails have scored his back I'm certain, but he doesn't say a word. He just keeps slamming his hips into me, hitting that secret spot within and dragging my orgasm out into oblivion until he comes, hot and pulsing inside of me. His body collapses on mine. His face is buried in my neck, where he continues to lick and kiss me tenderly while we both catch our breaths.

My senses start to return as my breathing calms and my world stops spinning. I've never in my life done something like that and instead of being alarmed, I feel relaxed and free. I've never been a risk taker or a fly by the seat of my pants kind of gal. I may be sorry later, but for now I see why so many people are. I release a relaxed sigh and caress the soft stubble of his hair. After a few quiet minutes, where all the world feels right he stands up and puts his shorts back on. He pulls me to my feet, and helps to brush the sand off. I adjust my clothing and put myself back together.

Garrett is the first to speak as he grabs my hand leading me back toward the hotel.

"I'm sorry I attacked you." He gives me a sheepish look that should annoy me, but instead I find endearing. How upset could I be with him when he just gave me the most powerful orgasm I've ever had?

I surprise him by smiling and saying, "Nah. I'm okay. I think I wanted it just as much as you did."

He studies my face for a moment, shakes his head like he wasn't expecting that answer, smiles back, and continues leading me back to the resort.

We don't say much following our encounter, but right after I push my sandals back onto my feet he takes my face in both of his hands and kisses me with lips so tender it makes my heart ache a little. It's the kiss you'd expect from a longtime lover, not some guy you just met and screwed on the beach. So, for that one brief second I pretend that he's the longtime lover not just some guy. Then I take a step back and let reality enter my thoughts again because I don't want things to be too awkward for us.

I'm sure this is common place for him, even if this is my first such encounter, so I paste a smile back onto my face and tell him goodbye. I waltz up to the bar, grab my stuff from Maxi the bartender, and walk back to my room without looking back at him. This feels a little bit like what I'd guess the walk of shame to feel like. I should be freaking out. The guy didn't use protection, who knows where he's been before, and he came in me. This leaves the possibility for disaster, but instead of worrying about that I fill up my whirlpool tub and soak, thinking about the sexy, stranger with the beautiful pictures and the super-hot body.

Chapter Three
Lisa

I awaken with soreness between my legs that I haven't felt in a long time and a lightness inside that's been missing in equal measure. I get up, throw myself together, and head downstairs for breakfast and coffee. Once I'm done with breakfast, I go back to the room and change into my running gear. Then I make my way down to the beach and start my morning run. I took up running a few years ago as a stress reliever and found it almost necessary to function after Matt died.

My long strides eat up the sand as I keep the steady pace I set for myself. I'm five-foot-six and most of that seems like legs. I'm sweating from the extra exertion of running on sand and the added humidity here. Seagulls scream above me as they circle the shoreline and the briny smell of salt water fills my nose. The beauty of the location makes it worth the added effort today.

On my way back, I spot Garrett with his camera further back on the beach by the sea grass. His focus is on a couple of kids playing by the water. I don't want this to be awkward. I may not be very experienced, but I know what a one night stand is, so I turn my focus back to the sand in front of me, finish my run, and go back to my hotel room without acknowledging him at all.

I shower and change. Then I head to the beach with

my iPod, towel, and a book. The smell of suntan lotion and warm sand drifts through the air. It's something that you only find at the beach. It makes me think of family trips to the Jersey shore when I was a kid and those thoughts make me smile. I spend time wading in the cool blue-green water and gathering shells to take home with me, until I'm ready to lay out.

I've been stretched out and relaxed for a couple of hours with my eyes closed, my ear buds in, and my iPod on when my overheated skin is tapped by a cold finger. I jump with shock and open my eyes to find the guy I rented the chair from holding a frozen drink with a little umbrella for me. I raise myself up on my elbows, yank out my ear buds, and tell this guy, "I didn't order anything."

He smiles at me and passes me a napkin with a note written on it and says, "This is a gift."

He shoves the drink in my hand and walks away. I sit myself up and open the napkin to read:

Lisa,

You are even more beautiful in the light than you were in the dark. I hope you are enjoying your day relaxing.

Garrett

I smile and look around, hoping to see him, but I don't. I take a sip allowing the frozen drink to cool my lips and throat as I swallow the tasty concoction, realizing it's a piña colada. Then pop my ear buds back in and spend the rest of the day reading a hot romance novel my sister suggested. In the late afternoon I head back to my room for a shower.

Tonight, I've decided to eat at the Hammerhead Grill. The fish tank in the restaurant is what brought me to this location, so I feel I need to check it out in person. I order the grilled jerk swordfish and sit back with my glass of white wine, admiring all of the colorful tropical fish swimming carefree in front of me. The tank really is more spectacular in person than it was on television. I take out my cell phone and snap a few pictures, which I attach to a text for my niece.

Garrett

It's mid-morning when I change out the lens on my camera and bring it back up to my eye expecting to capture the kids digging in the sand near the waterline when a pair of long, sexy legs enters my viewfinder. I lower the camera to get a better look only to realize Lisa is clad in short black spandex shorts and some kind of purple racer back spandex tank top. She is jogging along the shoreline, blonde hair shining in the sun as it swishes from side to side in her ponytail as she goes. I scan that perfect body from head to toe, noting every flex of lean muscle from her ass to her ankles. She's got a body that doesn't quit. *Fuck.*

Knowing what that body is capable of without clothes has me hard in an instant making for an uncomfortable situation since I've been sitting here taking pictures of little kids for the past half an hour. *Damn.*

I shove my camera into my bag and use it to shield myself as I head back to my hotel room. It's apparent that I need to take care of business myself before I can continue working. I hustle my way through the hotel lobby without drawing too much attention to myself.

A half-hour later I'm strolling back to the beach when I spy her again. This time her long, sexy body is stretched out on a lounge chair. Her eyes are closed so

I'm able to rake my eyes over her skin, resting on the swell of her perfect breasts, along her flat stomach, all the way down her super long legs. Perfection. I shake my head to clear it and move in the opposite direction hoping that the out of sight, out of mind theory will work for me today.

A couple of hours later, I've gotten a few more shots, but I know they are nothing to write home about so I pack my camera away and move back up the beach to the tiki bar area. Along the way I catch a glimpse of her again and groan out loud. As if I can't control myself, I pull out my camera and snap a few shots of her stretched out like a sun goddess before I shove it in the bag and trudge up to the tiki bar.

She was only one night, just one night. Leave it at that, Garrett. Keep walking. Don't be stupid. I keep telling myself over and over. By the time I get to the bar, I've decided that I can't let it go, not all the way, so I order her one of those frozen drinks she seems to like so much and scribble a little message on a napkin. Then I pay the guy in charge of the chairs and umbrellas to deliver it. I go back to my seat at the bar, order a beer, and listen to the live steel drum band they have playing up near the pool. The island sounds keep the mood around the resort jovial and relaxed, however I'm not. She's got me so spun up I almost can't sit still.

After a couple of hours I go back to my room and get cleaned up. I've stewed over this woman all day long. I haven't been able to think of anything else except the way her gorgeous body came apart beneath me last night. She let loose like no one I've ever been with before and that alone is sexy to me. I've decided if she's at the bar alone tonight I'm going for it again. I just won't make any pretty promises to her that I know I can't keep. The first place I plan to look for her is on the beach at sunset. I've never seen anyone enjoy it the way she does.

****

As my bare feet step from the wooden walkway into the warm grainy sand my eyes find her. The sun is slipping below the horizon at a snail's pace and she is once again engrossed in the view. I take those last few moments to admire the soft curves and long lines of her perfect form, realizing that I'd give my weight in gold if I could photograph her naked on this beach. The idea flitting across my mind has my cock stirring in my shorts. I should be snapping pictures with the camera in my hand, but I can't seem to grab a coherent thought long enough to do so.

With fluid grace she rises to her feet and brushes both hands along her bottom, brushing the sand off. She turns to walk my way and freezes as she sees me, a smile spreading across her face. I smile back and wait for her to reach me.

Damn, I want this woman. I can't remember wanting someone like this. Not ever. This time though I want her bare for me. No fabric in my way. Nothing but skin on skin. I want to feel every last inch of her and I plan to do just that.

Lisa

After a wonderful meal, I meander back down to the beach and park my butt in the soft sand anticipating another spectacular sunset. Today's colors are not quite as bold as yesterdays, but it doesn't detract from the beauty of it. It's not long before the sun disappears and the colors fade to black so I get up and dust myself off.

When I turn to go back to the hotel I notice that Garrett is standing by the walkway with a smile on his face and his camera in his hand. I give him a smile and a small wave. Surprisingly, he waits for me there.

"Want to have a drink with me?" The deep timbre of his voice sends shivers up my spine and memories of him moving inside me last night skate through my mind. I tilt my head, studying him for a moment. Don't most guys avoid seeing a one-night stand again? Not sure what to make of this, but I'm curious enough to find out, I take his outstretched hand.

"Sure. That sounds good." I smile and remind myself to relax and enjoy.

I slide my sandals back on and lead the way back to the tiki bar. He pulls a chair out for me at one of the high top tables and sits across from me.

"How was your day?" He asks, with a charming smile.

"Good, very relaxing. Thank you for the drink by the way. It was fantastic."

"My pleasure."

"How was your day? Productive?"

"Yes. I got some beautiful shots today and even had some time to swim."

The server comes over, takes our order, and walks away.

"So, tell me about yourself, Lisa."

"What do you want to know?"

"Anything, everything." He flashes me that sexy grin and my panties dampen in response.

"I live in Cincinnati. Born and raised. My family is all still there. I graduated from Ohio State University and I'm currently a social worker. No kids. No cats.

One dog, named Barry, after baseball great, Barry Larkin, and a lot of friends. What about you?"

I lift an eyebrow, waiting to see if he will answer. I think my quick no nonsense response surprises him.

"My condo is in Miami, but I travel so much that it's rare for me to see it. No wife, no kids, no pets. I'd love to have a dog, but I'm not home enough. My parents and my brother live in a little town about two hours north of here called Crystal River. It's where I grew up. I have a sister who lives with her husband and daughter on a horse farm in Ocala, also about two hours from here. I have friends scattered all over the world and I'm a freelance photographer."

"That must be fascinating. It would be my dream job if I had any talent behind the lens. I've been a social worker with hospice since I graduated college over ten years ago. My family doesn't know it, but I'm interviewing for a job with United Way in Orlando later this week. I need a change. If I get the job and accept it, my family is going to freak out. No one moves away. They all still live there. Grandparents, aunts, uncles, cousins, parents, sister, everyone. They may go away to college, but they all go back to Cincy to set up house."

I shrug and look at my hands, which are nervously shredding the napkin in my hand. When the server sets my drink in front of me I down half of it in one shot not giving myself the chance to even taste it. I look up to find a half-amused Garrett watching me.

"You okay?" he asks.

"Yeah, I just hate to disappoint them, but it's time for a serious change."

Garrett chuckles. "Being different is not a bad thing, Lisa. It opens you up to so many new things."

"That's what I'm hoping for. I've just been through so much and they don't even know the half of it yet. I'm hoping for supportive, but expecting a freak out."

The breeze weaves it's way through the bar area ruffling my hair as we talk a little more about some of the places he's been, how he got started in his career, and a little about his hometown. In a sweet gesture he tucks the hair that's flicking in my eyes behind my ear then cups my face with his palm and brushes my cheek with his thumb. My body stills and our eyes lock on one another. This one small touch sends heat snaking through my entire body. He must feel it too because he takes a deep breath and lowers his hand to one of mine sitting on top of the table. He takes it in his and rubs his thumb over the top of it as he continues our conversation.

After an hour or so of talking and little touches, he glances up at me through his lashes and asks, "Would you like to take another walk down the beach with me?" The grin that accompanies the question is devilish causing my nipples to bead and my stomach to dip.

I search his eyes for a moment before I give my response running through the pros and cons of a yes answer. If my instincts are correct, the night will be filled with more than beach walking. *Why the hell not?*

"Yes." I flash him a flirty smile and slide off of my stool.

We walk further down the beach tonight. We pass a few other couples and the same jogger from last night. Garrett's hand is warm around mine again and the butterflies in my stomach accompany me as we stroll. His voice is so deep it seems to rattle and stir all of my inhibitions loose. The farther we go the more I hope that I didn't misread things, that he wants a repeat of last night. Thank God I'm not thinking out loud. I sound like a hussy, but the things Garrett did to my body last night are more than just memories. Each touch is burned on to my skin, heating my flesh even now.

The anticipation is killing me. I can't tell if he's having the same reaction to me or if I'm fabricating all of this in my head, hoping for more than it is. My thoughts come to a screaming halt when he stops walking and pulls me into him. My gaze connects with his for a long quiet moment, the only sound is the waves crashing at our feet. His fingers brush my hair behind my ears and he gives me another tender stroke of his thumb across my cheekbone. I love the feeling this one little action of his gives me. I close my eyes as I savor the touch. His lips are soft against mine at first while his hands are slower, more deliberate. He's building this again, but it's much more controlled than last night. He's a master of seduction. Making me want this all the way down to my core, causing any remaining inhibitions to take a running leap into the ocean.

My hands caress his chest, around his shoulders and back down again across the ridges of his abs and I'm hungry for the feel of his skin against mine any way I can get it. There is no hesitation as I slide my hands under his shirt and with the lightest of touches explore the skin underneath. His body is warm and tight against mine and he lets out a soft groan at my touch.

I'm only a little tipsy tonight, far more aware of everything happening. It's a strange feeling, exciting and terrifying all at the same time. Instead of just dropping us to the sand he unbuttons my dress down the front at the slowest possible pace. I almost want to just rip it open for him. My patience is waning as my chest expands with each breath. He slips the straps over my shoulders and the fabric pools at my feet. Goose bumps rise all over of my skin in response to the feather light brush of his fingers on my shoulders and back as he unhooks my bra and pulls it off of me with a gentle tug, discarding it into the sand below us. I'm posed in the moonlight with only a small strip of soaked satin thong covering me. Instead of being self-conscious, I'm feeling wanton, reckless, and ready. So very ready.

Warm kisses are spread down along my neck to my breasts. He's paying special attention to the pebbled peaks with his lips and tongue. The soft lap with the flat of his tongue and light nip with his teeth are bringing me to the brink of orgasm. I can't control my reaction to him and as good as this feels I don't want to. He continues working his way down my body, sliding my panties down as he goes. He is making sure to touch every inch of me.

I take a deep breath in through my nose and allow the briny air to flood my nostrils. The memories of my childhood that this smell conjures will forever be replaced with scenes of this moment.

In a quiet, husky voice, he says, "I'd kill to photograph you naked in the moonlight. I'm not sure there is anything more beautiful on this Earth, than you right at this moment."

I'm glad it's dark enough so that he can't see my cheeks heat with happiness and a little embarrassment. I'd like to appear confident to him, not a little insecure, and battered by the knowledge that I was never good enough for the man I pledged my life to.

Matt and I were together so long that some of the passion you start out with when you're young was gone by the time he passed. Don't get me wrong. We still had sex. Good sex, but it hadn't been this steamy since the beginning. I haven't had a touch this reverent in a long, long time. He lifts one of my legs up and over his shoulder while his lips meet the apex of my thighs. His fingers spread the folds and his tongue makes a slow swipe from top to bottom and back up again teasing my sweet spot. A hum of pure pleasure releases from somewhere deep inside me as he repeats this motion.

"So wet. So ready for me," he rasps. With each pass, he adds more pressure. My fingers move across the short hair on his head, dragging my fingernails along his scalp while he works his mouth between my legs. I'm close to falling apart and he must notice the shaking in my legs because he stops what he's doing seeking eye contact and says, "Come down here with me."

He lays me out on the sand like last night except there are no clothes at my back and the sand cooled by loss of the sun is a sharp contrast to the heat of my skin. He places his mouth on the tender flesh between my thighs tasting me again, twisting his tongue around my sensitive bundle of nerves, licking from top to bottom, and then back again. My thighs are clenched tight and would probably be crushing him if his strong forearms weren't holding them in place. Ending the anticipation, he takes mercy on me, flicking his tongue in short quick strokes, rocketing me to a show-stopping orgasm that incinerates me. I grip harder, my back arched, my fingernails in his scalp with a cry of completion from my lips.

When I've caught my breath he crawls like a powerful jungle cat between my legs again and pushes his throbbing, hot shaft into me. My already sensitive cunt clamps around him and I cry out at the added pleasure his fullness brings.

The fire inside me ignites once more and I roll him to his back, never breaking our connection. I'm eager to move on him. I want to have some control as to where this goes. His hands find my aching breasts, touching and squeezing them with need, while I slide up then down with torturous slowness, until I can't take it anymore. His fingers pinch and roll my nipples with practiced ease and I grind harder on the down stroke. A hiss between his teeth brings my attention back to his face. The look he's giving me is one of a man losing control, concentrating to hold on until I make it there again. As my need builds, I'm unable to keep this slower pace. I increase my efforts, riding him hard to his climax. The flexing of his arms and chest drive me higher, as his hands clamp down on my hips helping to set the perfect rhythm. As his climax takes over, he presses his magic thumb to my clit and makes a swirling motion for the three short seconds it takes me to come again, crying out, louder than before.

My body collapses on his like a wet noodle and I take a few minutes to gather myself not wanting to move. The slightest adjustment to our current position could set me off again and I'm not sure I could take it. He pushes the mass of my hair over his shoulder, out of the way, and kisses the top of my head. Warm hands trail along the feverish skin of my back and arms currently being cooled by the ocean breeze. I inhale his musky scent mixed with the smell of our sex and wait for my body tremors to subside all the way. I imagine it'll take a while with three orgasms under my belt, but that's only a guess since it has never happened before.

"You are so damn sexy, Lisa. I had no intentions of seeing you again after last night, until I saw you running on the beach this morning. I spent the rest of my day trying to talk myself out of finding you and I'd almost convinced myself until I saw you all laid out under that umbrella. It was then that I knew I'd do anything to be with you again tonight. I'm not sure anyone has ever had that effect on me."

I stay where I am, sprawled across him, listening to his heartbeat, steady and strong in his chest. It brings me both comfort and excitement. I consider my words before I say them, knowing I shouldn't over-share.

My voice is quiet when I tell him, "I've never done anything like this in my life. I've only ever been with my husband, but I knew that what happened last night was a one-night thing so I didn't expect to see you either. I did notice you when I was running, but kept going, thinking I didn't want it to be awkward. You don't have to worry. I don't expect anything. I'm just enjoying this crazy, amazing fantasy for what it is."

"I'm glad you understand. I've never been in love. Never committed myself to another person. I just don't think I'm capable of it. I don't want to hurt you, but for whatever reason I couldn't stay away from you tonight either. You really are something special."

Even with his sweet words, I realize that the magic is over for the evening. I'm a little sad, but sated all the same. I stand up and start looking for my clothes while he puts his shorts and t-shirt back on. He lifts my hand, kisses my knuckles, and walks me back to the resort. This time before we part ways he kisses me long and deep, like he's claiming me, but I know that's not possible, not what this is about. It makes me a little blue, but there is no way I'll let him see that. I hold my head high and go back to my room without another word from him.

Chapter Four
Lisa

I'm pretty certain that last night is the last I'll see of Garrett, but it doesn't stop me from bringing him to dreamland with me. The guy was white hot in the sand. I'm certain it was never that good with Matt. It could be that Matt and I had grown too comfortable with one another after so many years. Or maybe he was worn out by his other escapades and didn't have any creativity or heat left for me. Matt was my one and only. Sadly, unbeknownst to me, I was not his.

That knowledge has caused me to question so many things about myself. The confidence that I carried all of my life was crushed by the weight of his infidelity. Being with Garrett, this sexy, strong stranger—not just once, but twice—has helped in the self-esteem department. When it was brought to my attention that Matt had been unfaithful, it made me wonder what I didn't have that he was seeking elsewhere. I've often wondered if I just sucked at sex, no pun intended, and instead of hurting my feelings, he found other partners. I'm not worried about that anymore. For the first time in a long time, I'm able to drag my thoughts away from Matt by replaying my time in the sand with Garrett.

Now that I'm awake early, the wet dream bringing me out of sleep earlier than usual and clogging up my thought process, I guess I can get up and prepare for tomorrow's interview. I'm meeting with a lady named Nancy about a management job with the United Way organization in Orlando. My family and friends don't know that I've even been looking for something new, somewhere new. If I get the job, I'll tell them, but if not I'll keep looking and tell them when the right moment presents itself.

I need a break from the memories of Matt that now feel false and the rut that my career seems to be in. I need a fresh perspective and a new mission in life. It's time for some self-empowerment. I've applied for several other jobs at various places around the country, but haven't heard anything back yet.

After I finish prepping for my interview, I beeline for the beach to get my morning run in. It's a bit overcast this morning and I make a mental note to check the forecast for the day. As I hit the home stretch on my return I notice that Garrett is in the same place he was yesterday. His camera is up to his eye and he is snapping away at a pelican standing in the surf. He must notice me because he lowers the camera and gives me his sexy, white smile. I wave and smile back, never breaking stride.

The cloud cover has broken up so I head to the beach afterwards and enjoy the Florida sun. Throughout the day, clouds start building on the horizon again, but as the afternoon wears on, the clouds become darker and the lightning flashes closer to shore. I pack up my stuff and head back inside the hotel. As I set my iPod and book on the bedside table I notice the light on the phone is blinking, indicating that I have a message, so I pick it up and listen.

"Hey, Lisa, it's Garrett. The hotel wouldn't tell me what room you're in so I could ask you in person. I guess I have to leave the message here. I was wondering if you'd be interested in having dinner with me tonight. I'm only here through tonight and to be honest I'd just like to see you again. You can call my room, number four ten, and let me know."

Hmm. This is an interesting development. A charming, stimulating, confident man is asking me to dinner. Should I dine alone as I have been the last couple of days or should I just go for it? I pick up the phone and dial his room with a smile on my face.

I try to hide the nervous shake to my voice as I say, "Hey, Garrett, it's Lisa."

A surprised but happy tone is detectable in his response, "Hey, sorry about the message, they are strict about the privacy policy."

"That's okay. About dinner, yes, I'd love to have dinner with you. What time should I be ready and where are we going? I didn't bring anything more than sundresses and shorts to wear."

"Is seven p.m. okay? I was thinking something casual. There is a bar and grille down the road that I hear is worth the visit. Will that work?"

"Sure. I'm in room seven ten."

I sit on the edge of the bed tapping my foot as he responds, "Okay, see you in a little while."

I hang up the phone and get in the shower. I have a few hours to get ready, but if I wash my hair now and it has a chance to air dry it looks so much better. My curls tend to frizz when hit with a blow dryer, even with the diffuser attached.

I end up being ready early so I park myself on the

balcony and watch the remnants of the storm drift back out into the Gulf. The rain cooled the air down quite a bit and I'm able to read, relax and enjoy the amazing view.

At seven p.m. sharp, I hear a knock on the door. I open it to find Garrett in a white button up shirt with the sleeves rolled to the elbow, khaki shorts, and deck shoes. He is the kind of guy who you'd expect to see taking a sail boat out from the local marina. The perfect Florida boy. I'm wearing a red halter-neck sundress with a white design across the chest that falls just above my knees and white, cork-heeled, strappy sandals.

He gives me an appreciative once over before saying, "Wow, Lisa, you look amazing."

I blush a little at the compliment and thank him. When we get down to the lobby there is a cab waiting for us.

"I have a rental car here, but I figured we'd be drinking and I don't drive even if I've had one glass."

At dinner, conversation flows well between us. He's easy to talk to and appears to listen well. He's funny and even a little bit sarcastic. He wants to know all about my job and the one I'm interviewing for. We both drink a little too much, but he never gets sloppy. I've been around men that get sloppy and ridiculous the more they drink. Thank goodness he's not one of them.

We take a cab back to the hotel and I invite him back to my room, unable to end the night without more of him. I'm playing with fire using my bare hands I'm sure, but I can't help myself where he's concerned.

Garrett

All through dinner she was teasing me, messing with the chemistry that we seem to have. She was subtle, but seductive. Every time she crossed and uncrossed her legs my eyes were drawn to the long, arousing expanse of skin and the edge of the hemline that was riding higher up her thighs. Every time she'd lean forward to wrap her lush lips around the straw of her drink I'd feel my dick twitch. When she'd reach up to fidget with her necklace her exposed cleavage would beckon my perusal. It was carnal torture sitting across from her tonight.

Her dress is feminine and sexy but not slutty in any kind of way. It gives just enough of a hint of what is beneath that you can think of nothing more than taking it off to get to the rest, but covers everything enough to be considered lady-like. I've had to ignore the urge to tell several guys at the bar to fuck off and find someone else to stare at, but I don't want to come across as a violent dickhead. By the time we slide inside the taxi I'm fighting a full-blown hard on. I pull her in close with my arm around her shoulders for the ride. Her hand moves to the high inside of my thigh where she draws lazy patterns on the outside of my shorts. It's all I could do not to moan out loud or beg her to move a little higher. In the short cab ride to the hotel I have gone from a semi-aroused physical state to long, strong, hard and ready.

Thank God, her skin is flush and her breaths are shallow making it obvious that she has noticed and is feeling the same way. In the elevator on the way to her room I grab her shoulders and pull her against me kissing her hard and deep, leaving her with a dazed expression as she exits the elevator. With the chains of public scrutiny shed as we enter the quiet hotel room we push through the door all over each other. We ravish each other as we travel to the side of the bed so we are facing the full length, wall-to-wall mirror. The natural smell of her skin calls to me on a soul deep level as I nip and lick the tender flesh of her neck. She goes nuts every time I do this. She trembles with obvious desire as I run greedy hands over the front of her dress. Her moans echo off the walls as I pluck at her straining nipples through the fabric. Visions of ripping the dress clean off of her body clutter my mind. I've never been more turned on in my life. She's hot as fuck and I'm ready to show her how crazy she makes me.

I bend down and help her slip off her shoes one by one then skim my hands up her thighs and over her perky ass. As I rise to my full height behind her I whisper in her ear, "Look up. Watch us, in the mirror. It's so fucking hot."

My eyes are trained on what my hands are doing in the reflection. I don't always have to be in control during sex, but I can feel the alpha male taking over tonight. I know my movements are strong, almost forceful, and demanding. I'm sure I'm being too rough, but I can't seem to control this. She makes me reckless with lust.

When my eyes meet hers in the mirror, a shiver runs through her body. I can feel it and my body reacts with a groan and a flex of my erection into her back. A moan escapes her, unlike any sound I've heard a woman make before, and she reaches back to stroke me through my shorts. I untie her dress and wrench it down over her hips onto the floor. Then I start to work on my shirt. Never breaking eye contact in the mirror I command, "Touch yourself. Over your bra, over your panties, do it now while you wait for me."

She seems a little hesitant at first, shyness filtering through the lusty haze of her expression.

"Come on, baby. Give me what I want," I whisper-growl to her and give her a playful nip on her earlobe.

With no more hesitation, she runs her right hand down her belly and over her black lace panties pressing down as she goes. Her left hand moves up to circle her erect nipple. Her head lulls back against my shoulder and she succumbs to the pleasure she's giving herself. This is so damn hot! I love watching her like this.

With her head back and her breath heavy, I can smell the sweetness lingering from the drink she had with her dinner and I lick my lips, hungry to taste her, everywhere. I drop my shirt near our ankles and my shorts follow right after.

She reaches back behind her again to find that I was commando under those shorts. Her cool, little palm wraps around the sizzling skin of my engorged cock and I thrust into her grip as a noise escapes the back of my throat. I'm impatient as I unhook her bra, letting it float to the floor and yank hard, snatching her panties clean off her body in one strong tug. I'm certain I've left a fabric burn, but she doesn't complain, she only presses her hips back against mine.

My heart rate is through the roof when I grip her arms and give her a little shove toward the bed. I'm beyond the point of control. I'm a slave to need and lust and her sexy fucking body. Her ass is round and raised as she crawls across the bed like I've commanded. I'm in heaven.

Lisa

Gone is Mr. Manners and here is Mr. Alpha Sex God. I crawl forward on my hands and knees, stopping only at his command. Despite the air conditioner running in the room there is no relief for my overheated skin. He positions himself between my legs and runs his hands over my back with a roughness I enjoy, down across my ass, and over my thighs. It's possible I'll combust just from his touch in this position, before he even penetrates me. It feels like I'm at his mercy.

I wiggle my ass at him with impatience and he smacks me hard right on the fleshy surface. I gasp and he rubs his palm over it, softening the burn. It stings a little, but I've got to say, I like it. It turns me on even more. He smacks me again on the other side making the sting even out and I give a little mewl in response.

I never thought I'd enjoy being spanked, but I'm about to beg for more when he steals my breath as he enters me in one deep, plunging stroke. I cry out and jolt forward a little. He yanks my hips back into place, strokes my back and waits. I wiggle my ass again, eager and impatient for him to move.

This pause, this waiting game he's playing, heightens my senses as I wait to see what he will do next. My muscles begin to tremble and my breath comes in short bursts. I don't know how much longer I can wait. My heart thrums like a trapped wild animal, my body is taut with passion. I've got a beast in me that's clawing to get out. Like a hungry lioness trapped in a cage. I clench my sex around him hoping to entice his movements.

After what feels like forever Garrett makes his move. He wraps my hair around his fist and forces my head up to watch in the mirror as he smacks my ass again and again before he begins a relentless, urgent rhythm. In and out, in and out. I'm crying out every time his hips are flush with my ass cheeks. My response to his sexual prowess will be a noise complaint from the front desk at any moment, I'm certain.

He pulls my hair a little more and guides my upper body so that my back is flush with his front. He never pulls out of me, only slows his stroke while he glides his hands over my breasts, my stomach, and down along my crease. Watching all of this play out in the mirror is the most erotic thing I've ever seen.

The bedside lamp although dim has every inch of our skin illuminated for this moment. My eyes are hooded, my skin is flush, and I can see the sweat beading on his brow and upper lip. With one hand between my legs, his talented fingers are circling my hidden pearl, while the other hand cups my breast and gives the tight bud a sharp pinch.

I turn my head to kiss him, needing the added contact. He plunders my mouth, with an aggressive, thorough kiss, like he can't get enough. My eager response must kill his reserve because without any warning I'm pushed with rough hands so that my chest is all the way to the bed, thrusting my behind higher in the air.

Right before he readjusts his body for a different angle he gives me a hard smack on each cheek with no gentle rub to follow. He's over top of me now and we are lined up like animals against one another allowing him to plunge deeper than he ever has before.

The visual in the mirror mixed with the feeling of him plowing into me over and over again ignites the flame that bursts from within my core only to spread out through every nook and cranny in my body like wildfire. I scream out my first orgasm, my body caged by his arms as he continues his rapid thrusting.

I've gone limp and my flimsy body is trying to slide down the bed, but he won't allow it. I grip the yellow comforter in both palms and squeeze as he clutches both of my hips and lifts, with impatient hands pulling my ass back up. His hand is back between my legs again and with every press of his fingers and every thrust of his hips, I fall further and further into continued orgasmic bliss. Animalistic moans climb up from within me until I'm hoarse and spent.

Finally, he comes with a rough growl and collapses on my back. We lay there, unmoving, our sweat covered skin, sticking to each other. His body is heavy with exhaustion, trapping me face down on the bed. I should feel squished and claustrophobic, but instead I feel sated and safe.

Best. Sex. Ever.

He chuckles and I realize I might have said that out loud. He peels himself off of me, goes to the bathroom, and returns with a wet washcloth. He's gentle as he cleans me up and I just lay there like the ragdoll I had on my bed as a kid. Lifeless and floppy. He throws the washcloth back to the bathroom floor and pats my butt.

"Come on, scoot up and over so I can lay with you."

I drag my tired body up, roll back the covers and hold them up for him to join me. He slides in and pulls me to his side. I lay my head on his chest while his arm wraps around me, rubbing back and forth in a sweet, gentle motion. It's a soothing gesture so I exhale and relax into him. The little dusting of coarse hair on his chest tickles my cheek and I can smell a hint of his cologne from earlier and the natural musk of his skin, a scent I'm fast growing addicted to.

"Was I too rough with you?" he asks, breaking the silence.

"No, not at all. I've never had it that way before, but I loved it."

"What do you mean, you've never had it that way? Weren't you married for a while?"

"Yes, but it just wasn't that way with Matt. He was never ravenous for me, I guess."

"He was a fucking idiot then. Sorry, I hope that doesn't offend you. But I've known you three days now and all I can think about is all the different ways I can fuck you. You are so damn sexy."

I smile at the compliment. "Well it's become apparent that Matt was too busy being ravenous for other women to act that way for me."

Garrett moves his head back so he can look into my eyes. "Are you serious?"

I avert my eyes so I don't have to face him when I answer. "Yes, I started finding things after he died that lead me to believe he was cheating on me. I have proof and now, one of the women is saying she's just had his baby. He screwed me over pretty good. He did a good job of keeping things quiet for years, but I would have found out now, that he knocked one of them up. I'm waiting for a paternity test to prove it so I can turn over half of his estate to the baby in a trust."

"Damn, Lisa. I'm sorry. No wonder you left town. That's a lot to deal with. What did your family say?"

"I only told my sister. I didn't want to upset my parents or his parents if I didn't need to. They don't need to know what kind of husband he really was unless it becomes a necessity. I should know by tomorrow or the next day. My lawyer is an old friend and he is handling everything for me."

"Well, he was an idiot. I've never been with a woman as sexy and uninhibited as you are. I can't seem to get enough."

His words light something in me that I didn't know was ever there. All of a sudden, I'm not feeling as tired anymore. I move my hand from his chest using slow, light touches down his stomach, over his flaccid cock, to his balls. Bravery in the bedroom was never my strong suit, but I'm feeling it now. I take the sac in my hand and give a light squeeze, running my thumb gently over him. He groans and I feel his thighs flex. He's growing at the attention I'm showing his most sensitive parts.

I maneuver my body down, in between his legs and take the soft flesh of his sac into my mouth humming as I go. I can hear his sudden intake of breath as I lick my way up his shaft and pull the blunt head of his cock in between my lips. His hands fist in my hair as I suck it all the way to the back of my throat. I repeat this motion again and again, swirling my tongue over the head as I move up.

I cup his balls with one hand while I stroke in tandem with my mouth using the other. I let his cock fall from my mouth with an audible pop, lick my lips and hold his gaze. His body is rigid and strung tight. I know he was getting close so I'm giving him a minute to settle back down. I'm teasing him just a little.

I move my mouth back to his sac and lick from the underside of the seam all the way up until I enclose the pulsing head of his cock in my mouth.

He hisses out his approval, "Fuck, yes, Lisa." His

eyes lose focus as I begin to move again adding more suction the closer I get to the top each time. Just before he loses control, he laces his fingers into my wild mane pushing me down harder. I gag a little but glance up to find him lost to the sensation. It turns me on to know I've made him feel this way so I get more creative with the licking and sucking.

He must not expect it because his body locks up and he blurts out, "Oh shit," as he tries to move me. I give him one final hard suck and I swear he growls as he lets go, coating the back of my throat. I swallow every last drop and crawl back up to the comfy place in his arms.

"Damn, woman. Are you trying to kill me? I didn't know blow jobs could be that awesome."

I giggle and settle in. He returns to stroking my back as I doze off.

I'm not sure what time it is when I wake back up, but I realize the light is off and I'm alone in bed. I sit up and look around the dark room noticing that the door to the balcony is open a little, letting the moonlight in. I grab a towel from the bathroom, wrap it around myself, and head for the sliding door.

Garrett

I stayed awake stroking Lisa's body with my fingertips until her breathing evened out and her body grew heavy with sleep. Then I slid out from under her, slipped on my shorts, and padded out to sit in one of the lounge chairs.

I'd been contemplating my next move for quite a while, when I heard her tentative voice inquire, "Are you okay?" She's standing just outside of the doorway in nothing, but a towel. *Damn.*

I give her a small smile, appreciating the way that towel looks wrapped around her body. I spread my legs apart and tap the vacated area. She sits down between them with the towel still wrapped around her and leans up against my chest. The sound of waves breaking is the only noise out here at the moment. The smell of salt more prevalent a night it seems.

"I'm okay. I was just thinking."

"Oh yeah. What about?"

"What time is your interview tomorrow?"

"Ten a.m."

"When you're done do you want to make a visit to Crystal River with me? I promised my parents I'd visit and I wanted to get some different shots for this project I'm working on, but I'm having a hard time leaving you just yet. It's only about an hour and twenty minutes from Orlando and when you're ready to come back here it's about a two-hour drive."

"You want me to come to Crystal River with you? Are you sure about that?" The skepticism is obvious in her voice.

"Yes, I am. I can take you out on the river to see some manatee. We can swim with them if you want. There is a spring on the river called Three Sisters that is breathtaking; I know you'll love it. We can kayak into the springs and I can get some pictures there. You can either come back down here tonight or stay with me there for a couple of days. I know you'll like my parents and the only issue with my brother will be keeping him off of you. He's a serious flirt. Come on, it'll be fun." I'm almost begging her and I'd like to kick my own ass for that, but I'm afraid she will say no if I don't beg.

She's quiet as she sits thinking about it for a few minutes. I kiss the top of her hair and hold her tighter. I'm hoping she doesn't have anything else planned.

"Sure, I'll go. I'll stay at least one night and then maybe head back here."

I let out a sigh of relief and give her a squeeze. "I'll give you the address and you can plug it into the GPS. If you have any problems you can call me. I'll give you the number before you pick up the rental car in the morning."

I scoop her up, one arm behind her back and one under her knees carrying her back to bed where I spend the rest of the night showing her just how happy I am. We never go back to sleep.

Chapter Five
Lisa

Interview complete. It's the longest one I've ever had, almost an hour and a half. Nancy and I hit it off right away, which helped with my nerves. She would be my boss if I get the job so I took that as a good sign. She says that she has four more interviews over the next several days and should make her decision by the end of next week. I thank her for her time and head back to the parking lot. When I reach the car, I call my sister and talk to her while I follow my GPS to Crystal River.

We talk almost the whole ride as I give her the abbreviated version of things with Garrett. At first she seems concerned but by the end she's excited for me. I give her the address of where I'm headed just in case there is an emergency and tell her I'll call her tomorrow. We hang up as I'm pulling in to the driveway of a beautiful two story yellow house with white shutters located right on the river.

Nervous energy zings through me as I open my car door. My feet haven't even hit the ground yet when the front door opens and Garrett strolls out followed by a good-looking guy about the same age. He's watching Garrett with an interested eye. When I step out of the car Garrett pulls me in for a big hug and a happy little twirl that lifts me off of my feet. I squeeze him back and he gives me a tender kiss grinning like a little kid with an ice cream cone. When he turns us around the guy is still standing there.

"Tommy, this is Lisa. Lisa, this is Tommy, my little brother."

Tommy and I shake hands and a bright smile spreads across his face. "Nice to have you here. Come on inside. My parents are anxious to meet you."

I look up at Garrett with a lifted brow. "Are they? What did you tell them?"

"Don't worry. It's nothing bad. I was just excited."

We enter through a small foyer into a great room with wall-to-wall windows facing the river. It's an incredible view. Garrett's parents are rising from seated positions on the couch as we enter. His dad is about his height with a full head of white hair. His face is a little bit weathered, but his expression is kind. His mother is shorter than I am with light brown hair with strands of gray interwoven throughout. It's pulled back in a ponytail at the nape of her neck. She also appears fit for her age. Her expression is more curious than anything.

I stick my hand out in front of me, first to his mom and introduce myself, then to his dad. Garrett still has his arm around my shoulders in a protective hold.

His mother breaks the silence. "Rhett, why don't you get Lisa something to drink?"

"Of course, what can I get you? We have soda, lemonade, coffee, water, sweet tea?"

"Sweet tea would be lovely... *Rhett*."

I giggle like crazy as he gives me a scathing look.

"My family has called me that for as long as I can remember. It's not my favorite." The look he levels his mom with makes me giggle more.

"What can I get the rest of you?" he asks.

Everyone shouts out their order and we all sit down. I'm assuming they leave the loveseat open for Garrett and I. Conversation is easy and I find that I like his family more than I expected too. They are so down to earth. They seem curious about me so I give them the basics and then we talk about my interview for a bit. It's midafternoon now and Garrett turns to his brother and asks, "Will you take us out on the boat before dinner?"

Tommy looks at him like he's nuts. "You can take the boat out. You know how to drive it. I don't have to tag along."

"Yeah, I know, but I want you to come."

"Oh, I see. You need someone to keep your woman entertained. Afraid you're too boring?" He says all of this with a mischievous grin. He's still smirking when his mom smacks him upside the head with a pillow.

"Watch your manners around the lady, Tommy."

I bust up laughing and slap my hand over my mouth when I realize how loud I was. This sends everyone else into a fit of laughter.

Garrett grabs Tommy in a headlock. "Come on, dumbass. Let's go. Lisa, do you want to change before we leave?"

"Um, yes. I'm thinking that a dress, heels and panty hose are not common boating attire."

After I change we take a tour of the river. The smell in the air here is less briny and more earthy. Like leaves, trees, moss, and mud combined. The sounds of crickets on the riverbanks and various birds overhead can be heard as we putter down the river. This place is beautiful and I can't wait to get out in the water tomorrow. We see one enormous manatee eating near the side of the canal. His tiny head and enormous body make him look rather awkward, but the whiskers and perfect, round nostrils give him a cartoon quality. He's so ugly he's cute.

About dinnertime we stop back by the house to pick up his parents and take the boat over to a local restaurant called Salty's. It sits right along Kings Bay and has a nice view of the sunset. I love that we can get right off of the boat and go inside here. I've never done that before.

We have a nice meal and good conversation while sitting on the deck in the warm evening air. His family is genial, polite, and intelligent. It turns out that Tommy went to University of Florida and got his MBA. Now he owns his own boat towing company. He has six employees and is doing well for himself. He has a small house a little further down the river on one of the canals. His parents are both natives to the area and both are retired from the local power plant. His dad has a part time fishing charter business and his mom helps out with a few local charities and keeps up with the house.

When we get back to his mom and dad's house they set me up in a room upstairs with a spectacular view of the river. As I gaze out the sliding glass door that opens to a balcony I'm entranced by the full moon hanging in the night sky and the little lights that dot the riverside where the houses are. In the center of the room is a king sized bed with big fluffy pillows and a sage colored comforter. Even better for me, there is a bathroom attached to this room.

Garrett takes the room across the hall. He told me earlier when we were alone that he wanted to be respectful in his parent's home so he requested two bedrooms. I was glad because I felt the same way. It's nearing midnight and I'm lying there, looking out over the water thinking about how different this life is than my life in Ohio when my door creaks open. Garrett's silhouette appears in the doorway as he enters and climbs into bed behind me.

"What are you doing here?" I whisper.

"I couldn't sleep. I won't do anything. I just wanted to hold you."

"What?" I ask, more than a little surprised.

"Yeah, this is a new feeling for me so don't ask. Just go with it."

I can tell by the sound of his voice he's grinning. "Okay." I smile to myself and relax against him.

He wraps his strong arms around me, pulls my back to his front, tangles his feet with mine and kisses my neck. "What is it about you that keeps me coming back?" His voice is quiet and serious.

I shrug, not having an answer for him.

"I wanted to punch my brother in the throat when I caught him staring at you today. Jealousy is also a pretty new emotion for me."

I don't know what to say so I stay quiet.

He rolls me over a little and kisses my lips. Then he moves my hair behind my ears and studies my expression in the moonlight. "Why aren't you saying anything?" His eyes narrow on me.

"I don't know what to say. I don't want to make this into anything more than what it is. It may not seem like it, but I'm pretty vulnerable right now and if I'm not careful my head will take this to a place it was never meant to go. I want to keep the memory of this time beautiful and perfect in my mind. These last few days have been some of the best of my life. I want to keep that."

"Fair enough."

He rolls me back to our previous position and I fall asleep like that. It's the best night of sleep I've had in over a year. I'm alone when I wake up to the shrill sound of my phone ringing in my purse. I hop out of bed with a thud and fumble around to find it.

I clear my throat and try to steady my voice, "Hey, Mark."

"Hey, Lisa. How's your vacation?"

"It's great. You must have gotten the results," Feeling more impatient than usual, I hold my breath waiting for the inevitable.

"Yeah. I'm sorry, Lisa," his voice gentles. "The baby is Matt's."

The tears roll down my cheeks, as I release the breath I was holding. "I knew it was going to be. Give me a minute, okay?" A sob breaks free and my whole body shakes with the force of my grief.

"Yeah, I'm sorry, honey."

It's obvious he dreaded making this call. The tone of his voice makes me believe he still held out hope this wasn't true, but I never did. I always knew in the pit of my stomach that Mariah was Matt's daughter. It takes me a few minutes to get myself under control. I sniffle and ask, "Did you get our offer drawn up?"

"Yes. Let's review it and you can tell me what you don't like. Five-hundred dollars a month for eighteen years, going back to the baby's birth four months ago. Then forty-thousand dollars for college or trade school and anything remaining in the trust will be paid out when she turns twenty-five years old. In the event of a catastrophic injury or major medical issue, like cancer, the lump sum can be used to help pay for medical expenses. It will all be subject to approval by the executor of the trust."

"Make it six-hundred a month and fifty-thousand dollars for college or trade school. I also think we should cover the medical expenses from the birth. Do you have the totals handy for that?"

"Approximately one hundred fifty thousand dollars."

"Wow! Is that normal? That seems excessive".

"Jill was in an accident the day she met you and was in the hospital for a month because the doctor was worried about the baby."

I didn't know that. I thought *I* was wrecked that day. In fact, I thought my world had imploded. I can't imagine what it was like for Jill. Not that I should care, but I guess hearing him recount what she had been through nudges my conscience a little. Maybe she didn't know he was married. It's possible I was quick to judge her and she wasn't ever out to scam for money so she could live easy. The possibility that she showed up wanting Matt to be the active father his baby was going to need only to find out he was married and dead had to be devastating. Adding a month long hospital stay and fear for her baby's well-being on top of it all makes me sad for her.

"Okay, do that and the remainder of the trust to be paid, half at twenty-five years of age and the other half at thirty years of age. I'm willing to give more per month, but we need room to negotiate. I don't want the little girl to want for anything. I just want to make sure it gets spent on her. And I'm hoping you'll agree to be the executor of the trust."

"Yes, I figured you would want that. I understand, Lisa. I'll contact Jill's lawyer and call you once they get back to me. Try not to think about this. Enjoy your vacation. All of this will still be here when you get home."

"I know. Thanks, Mark. Talk to you soon. Bye."

"Bye, Lisa."

I stand looking out on the view of the river. I'm grateful now more than ever that I wasn't left with any financial issues. Matt may have left me with more heartache than I could take but money isn't an issue. It wasn't until after I met with Mark about Matt's estate, that I became aware he'd taken a five hundred thousand dollar life insurance policy out on himself and named me the sole beneficiary. It surprised me that he'd done so since we had no kids and had paid off our home with his sales bonus four years ago. We've always been good with money, saving for a rainy day and never living beyond our means so the policy seemed excessive. Now I'm thankful for all of these things.

It takes me twenty minutes to dry my tears. When I make my way downstairs it only takes one look at me for Garrett to know something isn't right. He meets me at the bottom of the stairs, grasps my shoulders and looks into my eyes.

"What's wrong, sweetheart?"

"I got a call from my lawyer." My bottom lip is quivering.

I don't have to say anything else. He pulls me into a hug and I fall apart again. I should have realized that his family is standing off to the side watching us, but

I'm too busy having a nervous breakdown.

"I'm sorry," he whispers into my hair with a gentleness that I've not heard from him before.

"Thanks," I mumble.

He holds me like that until I stop crying and then escorts me to the table. When I realize everyone is in the room I'm quick to apologize. His mother places a gentle hand on my arm and tells me not to worry about it. Breakfast is quiet. I think his family is afraid to ask what's going on and I'm not sure if I should share. It's such an awkward situation.

After breakfast we paddle down the river in the kayaks and through a narrow water passageway to Three Sisters Springs. Trees line the sides of the spring area all the way around, shading most of the water except for the middle. The sand on the bottom is white giving it a magical appearance like something out of a magazine. Squirrels and birds can be heard back in the brush and up in the trees while the howls of swimmers ring out when their warm bodies hit the cold water. Garrett is right, this is breathtaking. He told me that the manatee pile into the spring area during the winter because the water is warmer here than in the river or the Gulf. Last year, over three hundred of them were packed into the spring at the same time. I can't even picture those enormous beasts piled in here three hundred deep.

The click of Garrett's camera is continuous as he takes it all in. After a few minutes he talks me into jumping in. Icy cold water covers my body as I take the plunge. Now I understand why people were screaming a few minutes ago. I swim away from where he is over the top of the headspring. It's massive compared to the smaller ones in the other section and a great big fallen tree lays at the bottom near the opening, acting as a sentry to any who dare get near it.

After I flop back into the kayak we paddle to Garrett's parents' for lunch. His dad says that the phone has been ringing off the hook since word got around that Garrett is in town so he decided to cook out and just have everyone over.

They invite me to stay another night and I'm having such a good time that I accept. The thought of walking away from Garrett makes my stomach knot up, but I try to push that thought from my mind. After the morning I had I don't want to even consider anything else that might cause me pain today.

By six p.m. there are about thirty people at the house milling around between the deck and the kitchen. His sister and her family didn't show up until an hour ago, something about a sick horse. His niece has been my constant companion since she got here. Her name is Olivia and she's an adorable four year old with the vocabulary of a teenager. Most of the guests are friends that Garrett has grown up with. It's obvious that most of them are surprised that he has a woman with him, but I down play it as us being friends. Everyone spends a lot of time telling stories about Garrett, most of them funny. I'm attentive as I listen feeling sorry for his mom and all that she had to endure with his childhood antics.

By ten p.m. everyone has gone home and I'm snuggled up on the loveseat next to Garrett watching a DVR episode of Jimmy Fallon, laughing my butt off. Garrett has his feet propped up on the table and me tucked under his arm. I'm feeling pretty content when he leans in and asks, "You okay?"

I turn my head to see his face. He's concerned. I pat his leg and reply, "Yes, I had a very nice day despite how it started. I enjoyed your friends and family. You're a lucky man."

His lips tip up at the corners and he leans in and kisses my forehead then goes back to watching the show.

An hour and a half later I'm lying in bed looking at the moon again dreading the goodbye tomorrow will bring. My stomach is in knots and I'm trying to fight off the tears. It was such a bad idea to come here. I've had an amazing time and I hate that I will never have that again.

Chapter Six
Lisa

The creak of the door echoes in the room once again as Garrett finds his way inside. He doesn't say a word, but it's obvious in an instant that he isn't taking the hands-off approach tonight. He snatches the covers off of me, strips my pants and panties off and positions his face between my spread thighs. I don't have time to say anything, only time for the gasp that escapes my throat as his talented tongue makes its first pass. I arch my back and close my eyes as I give myself a silent promise that I will catalog every last second of this to replay in my memory when I'm back in my bed alone.

He takes his time bringing me to climax, doing things to me I've only ever read about, and it's absolute torture having to be silent the entire time. It's a beautiful kind of torture though. When he's exhausted me with his mouth, he shifts up between my legs and slides inside of me slow and silent, which is in direct contrast to the fast and ferocious way he was eating me just moments ago. The flex of his muscles are visible in the moonlight as he keeps his pace slow, never breaking eye contact, leaving me breathless. My hips rise to meet him, our bodies in sync.

The spicy smell of his skin surrounds me as he takes me. Owns me. Controls my body with his. It's one of the most intimate moments I've ever had during sex. With my legs wrapped around the back of his thighs I'm urging his movements on. He rolls taking me with him allowing me to be on top. I rise and fall in slow, controlled strokes taking things at a snail's pace. I like to draw it out.

"Lisa," he growls.

He jackknifes up so we are now face to face and urges my feet around his back. We are nose to nose when I feel his hips flex the first time. He's so deep this way and the sensation has my head falling back. I can feel my hair sweep across my ass a second before he licks the shell of my ear and sucks on the perfect spot along my neck that drives me wild. Then he whispers, "Eyes on me, sweetheart."

I turn my face back to him and stay that way as we flex and roll against each other drawing us closer to nirvana. This position is sensual and intimate and I relish every second of it. His one arm is around me holding us tighter together while the other moves into the small space between us to find my breast and tweak the tip. I forget that we are in his parent's home as I cry out with abandon, squeezing my eyes shut.

He readjusts us so that he's above me again. His gaze is piercing through me. His expression unreadable and my heart contracts, unsure of what's happening between us as my emotions tangle within, as my body submits to his. His hips piston in and out of me as my world shatters like a dropped glass on tile flooring and somehow with his body, with his movement he puts it back together again. He groans his release never breaking eye contact with me.

When we've both finished, I feel the tears build and I fight to keep them at bay. Not wanting him to know that I've fallen in love with him. There is no doubt in my mind. I'm in love with Garrett and I'm terrified to leave him tomorrow. I don't want to feel the emptiness that I did after Matt died. I know this was never meant to be more than a few days at the most, but it has changed me and I don't think I'll ever be the same. My tears don't leak out until we are repositioned with my back to his front, legs tangled together like last night.

Thank God he passes out because I don't want him to know that I'm crying myself to sleep. So many things have happened. Starting with the confirmation that Matt has left a baby, that's not ours, in this world. Followed by a day filled with family and friends of the man I shouldn't be falling in love with, and ending with the most sensual lovemaking I've ever experienced. I know Garrett has to fly to New York for work, while I have to go back to my vacation in St. Pete. This has been the best week of my life and I hate for it to end, but I guess that's just the way life goes. Or at least that's what I tell myself.

My heart aches with the thought of living without him, but he's been honest all along about not wanting more. It's my own fault that I'm feeling the way I am now. At least I get to say goodbye. With Matt I never got that, which is part of what hurt so damn bad.

Garrett

Coward that I am, I pretend to sleep while she cries. My arms are already around her and the gentle shake of her body as she fights the emotion guts me. I know if I acknowledge her pain then I'd also have to face the feelings that have grown during this week and that is not something I'm willing to do.

After hours of watching her sleep my fingers ache to touch her one last time so I give in tracing the curve of her breast with a lazy finger, making light swirling motions around her nipple. It tightens in response and I roll it between my thumb and forefinger. I repeat the process of trace, touch, roll and this time am rewarded with a sleepy mewl, while her hips tilt back against mine. I press my cock against her ass seeking more friction. My fingers trail down over her ribcage, over the curve of her hip, and down to the lips of her pussy. As soon as I make contact with her sweet spot, she starts panting and begging me to fuck her. God, I love that.

"Please, Garrett, fuck me, fuck me, please," she whispers louder than I'm sure she means to. I continue to stimulate her until her body stiffens and shakes with the force of her release. After her body becomes rubbery with bliss, I remove my fingers, bringing them to my mouth so she can see and hear me suck her cream off of them. I give her the groan of a starving man.

I nudge her top knee forward and enter her in the spoon position. Pulling her hips against me, I rock in and out of her, the motion slow at first, allowing the tension to build. I'm grinding against her ass each time as I feel her hips move back against mine. When I can't take it anymore, I flip her on to her back and place a pillow under her hips for leverage. I tug her legs over my arms as my hands plant themselves on either side of her ribcage. I penetrate her soaking wet passage. I'm surging with the intent to go deeper than I ever had, which draws a keening sound from her that I hadn't heard until now..

Almost as if it's just a teaser, I pull out, lean down

and suck her sensitive cherry tips into my mouth. One at a time, I'm fanning the carnal fire already burning between us and the way we are together it won't be long before it spreads like a wildfire out of control.

Once I have her squirming and whimpering I readjust her legs over my shoulders and hammer back into her. Our bodies are working together like a finely-tuned machine. Building a climax that scorches through me from my balls all the way up my spine. Even as she thrashes beneath me I continue to work until every muscle I own tenses up, my eyes close tight, and I explode in a rush of hot fluid inside her.

That was the most powerful orgasm I've ever had and it rocks me to my core. I roll off of her, my legs weak from exertion and stumble to the bathroom. I wet a washcloth and clean her using as much tenderness as I can. Then I crawl back into bed and lay on my side with my head propped in my hand as I examine her, never saying a word.

Melancholy like I've never known before pulls at my gut, twirling and tumbling until I'm weighted down by its effect. Realizing that I feel something for her I've never felt before I give her a gentle smile as her eyes take in my every expression. I sweep tender finger strokes over all of her skin, from her hair to the tops of her thighs. It's almost like I'm memorizing every last dip, curve, and line of her skin. The gentle petting seems to lull her back to sleep.

Once I'm certain she's asleep, I slip out of bed and take one last look at my beautiful Lisa. The slight ache I've been feeling in my chest all night expands and consumes me. I've never felt this before and I hope I never have to again. I place one chaste kiss on her cheek and leave the room without a sound.

I go to my room and change my flight to an earlier one. Then I sit down with a pen and paper to once again take the coward's way out. I'm a real asshole for leaving this way, but there is no way I'll be able to say goodbye and watch her heart break like I know it will. I never wanted to cause her the pain that her husband did and if I stay until she wakes up it will happen. I'm not the kind of man who settles down and a woman like her deserves someone who will.

My mom meets me at the bottom of the stairs and I'm a little startled by this. It's early even for her. To be honest I was trying to avoid my parents too. I knew how they would feel when I made my decision. I never should have brought Lisa here. I should have said goodbye in that hotel room down south.

"Don't do it, Rhett. You'll regret it." The warning in her tone evident.

"My flight got changed, Mom. The client needs me there earlier than expected. I didn't want to wake her. I wrote her a note. Can you give it to her when she wakes up?" I avoid eye contact knowing she'll see through me. She knows me better than I know myself sometimes, which on a normal day is a good thing. *Today*? Not so much. I hand her the letter and before I can move toward the door she pulls me into a mom-hug and holds tight.

With a shaky voice she says, "Rhett, she's the one. I know it, you know it, we all know it. Don't make the mistake of a lifetime and let her go. You'll be sorry. I know you will. Please listen to me for once, son."

I squeeze her a little tighter and let go. I turn on my heel and stride toward the door picking up my camera bag and pulling up on the handle for my suitcase. With my hand on the doorknob I say, "I'll never have what you and Dad have. I've always known that about myself. I'll just end up hurting her and she deserves better than that. I love you, Mom. I'll come back when I can."

"You think by leaving now you are saving her from hurt? You can't be that dense, son. She's head over heels for you. Please stay." Her voice cracks and I know from experience that tears follow that sound.

"Mom, I can't stay. It will be better this way. At least she will be mad enough it won't hurt. It was never meant to be for us. I'm not even sure why I brought her here."

"I do. I know why you brought her here. I just wish you could see it."

I could hear my mom crying as I close the door behind me knowing that I'll be breaking more than just her heart today.

Lisa

I wake up a little blurry-eyed which I'm sure is a combination of the tears I'd shed and the lack of sleep. Daylight is peeking in the window and the aroma of sex is all over the sheets that surround me. I can feel myself smile until I notice that the bed is empty. I guess Garrett went downstairs again or back to his room. I get dressed, brush my teeth and finish packing. When I head downstairs I realize it's more than quiet in the house. Wondering if I'm the only one up, I head for the kitchen. What I see puzzles me a little.

Garrett's mom is sitting on a barstool at the counter, full cup of coffee in front of her, an envelope next to her, and a very sad expression on her face.

Through the windows, I can see his dad facing the river, hands on the dock railing, looking out over the water, motionless. No Garrett and no Tommy anywhere in sight.

I hesitate before I flash her a smile, knowing that something is off, but not sure what. "Good morning, Sandra."

She puts on a small forced smile and says, "Morning, sweetie."

"Garrett still sleeping?"

She doesn't answer right away, just stands up and walks toward me with the envelope. She places her hand on my arm and says, "He's gone. He loaded up a couple of hours ago, said he had a last-minute change in his schedule. He asked me to give you this."

I tilt my head to the side before I choke out, "He, he, left? Already? Why didn't he wake me? I would have left, too."

She shrugs and I can see the tension in her shoulders and the nervousness as she swipes her fingers over the envelope she's holding in front of her. It's like a smack to the face when I realize what's going on. When he woke me up in the middle of the night, that was my goodbye. He chickened out. Couldn't even say goodbye. A wave of shame crashes into me and the room feels hot. Dizzy doesn't describe the sudden onslaught of spins my head has going on. I can't believe he left me here. I shake my head trying to clear the muddled mess of emotions that are clogging my brain up.

"I'm sorry, I'm sure I'm holding you up from starting your day," I whisper trying to contain the overflow of heartache that's bubbling to the surface.

I'm getting frantic. I'm reeling from having all of that amazing sex last night to being left here without even a goodbye. Who does that? Takes you to their parent's house and then leaves you there without a goodbye, without anything? I'm thinking I might hyperventilate and I don't want his mom to see that. It's odd, but I'm feeling like I did the night that Matt died. Shocked, empty, scared and crushed with the grief of losing someone else that I love. Gone. No goodbye. What the hell?

I take two steps backward deciding to flee the situation, trying to save face. "Well, let me just pack my stuff up and I will be ready to head out myself."

I can hear my voice crack on the last word, but before his mom can question me I start to back out of the room, not taking the envelope. I can't imagine what it has to say. I just know I feel like an idiot for all of this. I shouldn't have come here. I should have let goodbye happen in St. Pete a couple of days ago. I knew I was falling for him and once again I've picked someone who doesn't want me.

I keep rambling as I go. "I don't want to miss a day laying on the beach so taking off now is the best idea. Thanks so much for your hospitality, for showing me your town, and letting me stay here. I had a lovely time."

I'm trying to get out of there before I have a major breakdown. I can feel it rising up in me like a volcanic eruption, over all of this unnecessary pain from a guy I've known less than a week. It's official that I've lost my mind. I hustle back upstairs and gather my things, so thankful that I'm already packed. As I come back down with my suitcase in one hand, purse slung over my shoulder, keys jingling in the other hand, both Sandra and James are standing there waiting, looking uncomfortable.

I clear my throat and give them both a shaky smile and a quick hug. I thank them again and propel myself out the door. I'm trying to save face even though I'm certain they can see my heart breaking before their eyes. I've never been a good actress.

As I'm loading my bag, James comes out to the car. His deep voice grumbles beside me. "Lisa, he's just scared. It doesn't excuse what he's done, but I know my son. He's scared. That boy has never been in love in his life and he is with you. He's never brought anyone home with him and never looked at another woman the way he looks at you. I'm sorry he's a coward. I thought I raised him better than that, but he'll come around."

"James, I'd love to believe everything you've said, but the truth is I knew this was short-term. I just met him Monday. I've been through a lot in the last year and should have known better than to let it get this far. I'm an intelligent person, I just seem to have lost that somewhere along the way. Thank you so much for welcoming me into your home. I enjoyed myself so much with your family and friends."

I slide into the driver's seat as tears are pooling in my eyes and I know I'm losing it. James catches the car door before I close it all the way, sets the envelope in my lap and kisses my cheek.

"It only takes a moment to fall in love, honey. I fell in love with his mamma the first time I saw her. She hadn't even spoken a word to me. Take care of yourself. He'll come around. I just hope you haven't smartened up by then. Drive safe." Then he shuts the door and watches as I click the seatbelt into place and back out of the driveway.

I cry for half the ride back to St. Pete. By the time I get back to the hotel I'm exhausted and heartbroken. I spend the rest of the evening with a bottle of wine I bought from room service while I sit on the balcony, drowning my heartache. I spend some of that time crying and some of that time being pissed at myself for being so vulnerable and stupid.

By the next day I've made up my mind to shove Garrett, and my time with him, in a folder marked DO NOT OPEN and file it in the back of my brain. That's the only way I can try to relax for the last couple of days I have here.

I text my sister to let her know I am alive and back at my hotel. She asks about Garrett and I blow her off by texting: *Vacation fling. It's over. He's gone back to work. Talk to you when I get home. I'm headed for the beach. Love you.* Then I shut off my phone and go to my lounger on the beach.

****

This morning as I'm about to leave, I open the envelope and I feel like I might get sick. I'm afraid of what it will say. Too much or too little, either way it's not going to make me happy, but I have to know what it says.

Dearest Lisa,

I know I'm a coward for leaving you this letter instead of waking you up. I had a schedule change and have to be in New York earlier than I expected. I had a wonderful time with you, better than I deserved. Commitment has never been my thing and I wasn't sure how to say goodbye to you. That's how you ended up in

Crystal River in the first place. I should have said goodbye to you in St. Pete, but couldn't bring myself to do it.

You have been through so much already and I couldn't be another person to add to that. It killed me to see you sad, even if only for a moment.

I know that life for you will get better. You are making changes to ensure that happiness and are stronger every day for it. You are an amazing woman and deserve a man equally as good to stand at your side. It's unfortunate, but I'm not that man. I'm sure you figured that out by now. I hope you enjoy the remaining days of your vacation.

Take care of yourself,

Garrett

Well, there you go. I stuff the letter in my suitcase; wipe the tears from my cheeks and head for the airport shuttle. A few hours later I'm getting off of the plane in Cincinnati. As I'm waiting at baggage claim, I get a call from Nancy at United Way, informing me that I got the job. I accept without thinking twice. She's giving me three weeks before my start date. At least something good came from this trip. Next, I listen to a voicemail that Mark must have left on my phone during my flight letting me know that Jill accepted the offer as it is and he needs me to come by and sign paperwork this week. I'm a little surprised that she accepted without a counter offer, but am so grateful to have something go smoothly for a change.

Chapter Seven
Lisa

I've worked a full day and am now nervous as I settle on the edge of the couch in the living room with Matt's parents, his brother, Steve, Steve's wife, Mary, his sister, Tara, her husband, Bobby, and Matt's oldest brother, Johnny.

After I got home from the airport, I scheduled a meeting with Matt's whole family for the next night, followed by one for my own. I also typed up my resignation letter effective two weeks from today.

I inhale pulling the air deep into my lungs trying to calm myself before I start. "First of all, let me say that I'm sorry to do things this way, but I couldn't figure out a better way to do it."

They're quiet as they all watch me with guarded, but curious eyes. These people have been my family for the last sixteen years and I hate to have to do this to them. I take another deep breath and exhale. Then I blurt out, "Matt had an affair, well to be honest, more than one, but my focus is on this particular one."

There is an audible gasp from pretty much everyone and Steve jumps to his feet like he's about to protest.

I turn sad eyes to him, as I say, "Steve, I wouldn't come here to tell you any of this if I didn't have irrefutable proof. I also wouldn't come here with these accusations if I didn't have a good reason. I'd rather you all stayed ignorant about his flaws, but none of us has that option any longer.

"Matt has a baby. A little girl, named Mariah, who is a little over four months old now. Jill, her mother, showed up on our doorstep pregnant about six months ago with these claims. She didn't know Matt died. It was apparent that she told him a couple of days before he died and just thought he'd abandoned them. Naturally, she was wrecked and very pregnant when I met her. I was a mess, too, and just couldn't deal with her at the time. I took her number and told her I'd call her in a day or two.

"I contacted Mark, our lawyer, and asked him what I should do. He suggested that I get a paternity test done after the baby was born to confirm. Several weeks ago, Jill agreed to get the test done and it came back positive that Matt is her dad. I found out while I was on vacation. I had Mark make an offer to share the estate and half the profit on the sale of our house with Mariah."

Tears are running down everyone's faces, including mine. I look up to where Steve's still standing and the anger is as evident on his face as clear as the heartbreak is on mine. He storms out of the room and slams the backdoor. No one else moves.

"I'm not here to cause trouble. I came here to give you Jill's contact information. I think you should get to know her and be a part of Mariah's life in any capacity her mom will let you. As much as it's broken my heart to find out all the things I have about my husband, I still think this could be a good thing for you all. You are a loving, close family and she is going to need to have one of those in her life and she's going to need someone to tell her stories about her father so she at least knows something about him. I've already gathered up all the pictures of Matt for Mariah to have when she gets old enough. Maybe you can share more."

I explain the way the money is going to be distributed to Mariah so they know what I've done and why I've done it that way. They're all in shock.

His sister asks, "Why would you give this woman the money he left you, especially after he cheated on you?"

"To be honest if it was just Jill, I'd never give her a cent, but it's not. I'm giving it to Mariah. No matter how much I hate it, she's his flesh and blood.

"At first, I was raging mad, but now I'm just heartbroken. We had what I thought was a beautiful, happy life, but apparently he wasn't as happy as I was. He went looking elsewhere, often, for something else. I found letters, notes, voice mails, and texts from several different women. I can't even confront him about it now. I just have to live with this knowledge and know that I was never enough for him."

Tara rushes over to hug me while I cry. His mom and dad are still silent except for some sniffles. I think the news has wiped everyone out.

"No matter what Matt did or didn't do, I loved him, still love him if you want to know the truth, and I still love all of you. I hope this won't take me out of your lives, but I understand if you feel it needs to. I also want you to know that yesterday I accepted a job in Orlando, Florida with the United Way. I have to report in three weeks. I'm hoping to leave town in two weeks and get settled down there before I start my new job. If you all are up for it, I'd like to see you before I leave. I'm on my way to my parents' house to tell them, too." I squeeze Tara's hand and stand up. She follows and pulls me in for a big hug. Her husband is next.

Johnny who hasn't said a word yet kisses my forehead and whispers in my ear, "My brother was a dick. I'm so sorry."

I don't say anything. I just pat his cheek fondly and give him a sad watery-eyed smile. Then I hug his parents. Before his dad steps out of the hug, he whispers in my ear, "I'm so sorry. I thought I raised him better than this."

I back away a step and say, "Matt is the only one at fault here. You raised him better than this it's true, but none of this is your fault."

He gives me a sad smile and lets me go to my car. Steve doesn't come back inside before I leave, so I figure that will be the last I see of him. It breaks my heart further. He and I had been friends longer than Matt and I were together, but I can't help how people react. I'm still not sure why he reacted the way he did. It wasn't like the claims weren't proven.

Telling my family everything is much more difficult because the focus isn't on them having a relationship with Mariah. It's about what Matt did to me and how I'm dealing with it. My family is pissed that I didn't tell them the day Jill approached me and that I went through this alone. They also weren't happy that I'm giving away half of everything to 'the kid' as they put it. I told them the same thing I told Matt's parents and that I didn't want to discuss it anymore right now.

Then I set the room on fire with my announcement

about moving to Florida. You'd have thought I committed a cardinal sin. I knew it was going to be like this though, so I just answer their questions and tell them as much as I can. When I can't take any more of the interrogation, I excuse myself for the night and agree to come back the next night once the dust has settled.

I go back to my empty house and start to pack my suitcase. Thoughts and emotions whirl in my mind like winter winds. I pause in front of my dresser to look at the photo of Matt and me taken the day we closed on this house. We're holding the *Sold* sign together and smiling at each other. We were so happy and in love, at least I thought we were. Now I'm left wondering if any of what we had together was real.

I turn back to my suitcase, my thoughts shifting again. This is the first time that I will live away from everyone I know. When I was in college, Matt was with me and so were a lot of my friends. In Florida, I'll be completely alone. Although I know I'll miss my family and friends, I'm excited about this fresh start. Besides I'm not going alone, Barry will be by my side. Here in Cincinnati everything reminds me of Matt. I'll never be able to move on if I stay.

I'm also glad I turned the burden of Matt's transgressions over to his family. I no longer have to carry that with me. The knowledge of his betrayal will never go away, but finally sharing it with our families allows me to move on.

Finding and losing Garrett now feels like the harder thing to deal with. Sadly, it's been easier to let go of Matt and to face the challenge of a new job and living in a new town. How do I forget about Garrett and our amazing yet brief time together when the pain is still so real in my heart?

Tired of heavy thoughts I grab the remote from the night stand to turn on the TV. I locate a sitcom to help divert my thoughts to a happier place as I finish packing. Then I look up the number for a moving company to pack everything else. I send a text to my friend Alison, who is a real estate agent and set up a meeting with her for tomorrow after work.

****

A brisk autumn wind whips through my hair as I load my suitcases in the trunk of my car. When a truck pulls up behind me I turn around to see that it's Steve. I hadn't seen him since the night I dropped the bomb on his family and was kind of afraid I never would again. It hurts my heart that our long-time friendship may be over because of Matt's mistakes.

He walks over to me with a sheepish expression, looking more at his feet than at me. Spitting mad, my sister barrels up behind me, ready to do battle in my defense. "Why're you here Steve? Weren't you a big enough dick to Lisa already? She doesn't need any more shit to deal with."

I turn to her calmly and say, "Chill out, April. I appreciate you having my back, but I can handle this. Give me a few minutes, okay? If I need you, I'll call for you."

She nods her agreement, but isn't happy about it. She stomps back into the house slamming the door behind her.

Steve speaks first. "I thought he was cheating on you that last year before he died. I confronted him several times about it, but he always denied it. We didn't speak for a few weeks over it. I knew the truth and I was pissed as hell at him. I just couldn't prove it and wasn't sure what I'd do if I could. He was my brother no matter how stupid he was."

"I'm glad you were looking out for me in confronting him. I had absolutely no idea what was going on."

"Lisa, I was in love with you all the way through school. When my brother asked you out and I found out, we had the biggest knock-down, drag-out fight we'd ever had. He knew how I felt about you, but didn't back off. He was a selfish son of a bitch, so he knew I'd go ape shit if I found out he hadn't done right by you."

I'm feeling slightly ill, looking bugged-eyed, and shocked. "Why didn't you ever tell me?"

"I was afraid to lose the friendship we had if you didn't feel the same. You meant so much to me."

"Oh, goodness, Steve. I would have gone out with you. You were my first, real crush. I just thought I wasn't your type. I ended up falling in love with your brother, but I liked you first." I give him a half smile, meant to smooth the waters. "But, if you had asked me out, you wouldn't have met Mary, and I see the way you look at her. She is who you were meant for, but I feel a little better knowing you did like me back then."

He laughs a little and pulls me into a big ol' bear hug. "You'll always be my friend and I'll always love you like a sister. Don't disappear. I know why you have to leave, but don't stay gone forever."

"I won't. I love you, too. Promise me that you will make an effort with Mariah. Don't take Matt's dumbass mistake out on that little girl. I have no idea what her mother's family is like, but she's going to need an uncle like you around. I saw a picture of her. She's cute. She has Matt's eyes, your eyes." My voice catches a little at the admission. "Make the effort, no excuses." I stab my finger into his chest to punctuate my point. Then I lift up on my tiptoes and kiss his cheek. He smiles a little and strides back to his truck to drive away.

An hour later, I load Barry up in the front seat next to me. For the first twenty minutes of the drive his stubby little tail wags excitedly as he watches out the window. By the time we're in Kentucky he rests his fawn-colored face in my lap. His squishy jowls push up giving him a cartoon quality and his big tawny eyes close so he can sleep as I drive. Within seconds his doggie snores fill the car so I turn up the radio a little and settle in for the journey.

It only takes me a couple of days to find the perfect little house. It's located two blocks from Lake Eola in a renovated area of downtown. There are quaint little shops, a few restaurants, and a nice park within walking distance. Three weeks later I close on the house and Barry and I move out of the hotel we've been staying in and into our new home.

It's a three bedroom, two-bath place with a little backyard and a cute front porch. It's an older house that was gutted and remodeled two years ago. It's perfect. Now every morning I can walk Barry before work and every evening I can take him running with me around the lake. Well, I can start that as soon as I'm feeling better.

Last week, I started feeling like I had the flu. To be honest, I haven't felt one hundred percent since Garrett left me at his parent's house, but in the last week I've been nauseous all day and achy all over.

Even with all of the positive changes, I've been fighting melancholy that seems to have settled in my bones. I think between having to fill everyone in about Mariah and getting ditched by Garrett something in me kind of broke. Something I'd been able to hold together even through Matt's death and the year that followed. I have to figure out how to learn from the experiences of the last year and make positive choices for my future. Getting settled in my new house and embracing my new career will be a good way to do that.

Garrett

I've been in New York for a month and I'm over it. Too many people, too much noise and it's too damn cold. I'm finishing up a job here and headed to Colorado next. More cold. I've been out a few times with friends, but ended up leaving early every time. I haven't been with anyone since Lisa and to be honest I'm just not ready. I wish I could just shove her out of my mind and find physical release with the nearest, willing, beautiful woman, like I always did before but my libido has checked out on me.

I thought that once I finished editing the pictures I took of her on the beach and at the springs, I'd be able to let her go. Wrong. So fucking wrong. I never meant for the council to see the pictures of her, but when they did those are the only ones they wanted. They wouldn't take no for an answer so I had to hand them over. I never got a signed release from her so once they cut me a check, I'll I have to track her down, and send her half the money.

Every time I see her face or the lush curves of her body my heart aches more. I'm talking a bona-fide searing pain right in the middle of my chest. I'm sure time will take care of it now that I'm done editing the photos. That theory would probably be convincing if I didn't have copies on my computer and phone that I can pull up at any time and often do. Turning off my computer, I groan as I think about another night alone in my bed.

****

It's two weeks before Thanksgiving and I'm in southern California when payment for the *Enjoy Florida!* campaign shows up in my account. My fingers fly over the keyboard of my laptop looking for the phone number to United Way of Orlando. She hadn't gotten the job when she was with me, but she felt confident that she would. Time to find out the verdict on that.

A woman with a high-pitched, cheerful voice answers. "United Way of Orlando, How may I direct your call?

"Is Lisa Browning in the office today?"

"Yes, sir. May I have your name, sir?"

Bingo! A smile spreads across my face for the first time in weeks realizing that she got the job she wanted.

"John Smith," I reply, not giving my real name for obvious reasons. As soon as she transfers the call, I hang up the phone and write down the mailing address from the website. Then I proceed to write a letter, which takes me three tries to get right. After going to the bank to get a cashier's check for half the profit from the photos, I take my flash drive to make copies of the prints of her. I get the first one I took of her at sunset, matted and framed which takes a week, I bundle it all up and have it shipped. Estimated date of delivery is the

Monday after Thanksgiving.

Lisa

I decide that I want to go home at Thanksgiving. I still don't know anyone here except the people at work and our office is closed on Black Friday so that will give me a four-day weekend. It will also make my parents happy. I board Barry at a local kennel until Monday and take a flight north. My sister is picking me up at baggage claim so I'm working my way through the crowd to find her. My eyes are roaming the walls looking for a bathroom sign along the way when a billboard-sized sign on one of the walls of the airport stops me dead in my tracks. It's an eye-catching beach scene during a brilliant, pink, purple, and orange sunset with a gorgeous woman seated in the sand alone, enjoying it. She's mostly in profile, but her features are clear. At the bottom it says simply, "*Enjoy Florida.*"

I can't move. I look around to see if anyone else is staring at it like I am. Total attention grabber. It's the picture that Garrett took of me at sunset and it is spectacular. When I finally snap out of it, I grab my phone and take a picture of the billboard. My sister is never going to believe this.

Still in shock, I give up on my quest for the bathroom and hustle down to baggage claim where I find her waiting. As soon as I get in the car I tell her all about it. She even pulls over to the side of the road to see the picture I've taken.

"Lisa, this is crazy beautiful. Did you know he was going to use one of the shots of you?"

"No, he never said a word. I haven't talked to him since the night before I left Crystal River."

"Can he use the picture without your consent?"

"Probably not, but I'm not mad. A little hurt that he couldn't tell me he planned to, but in the grand scheme of things, especially considering how he left, this isn't a big deal to me. If the picture was ugly or from an unflattering angle I may be trying to hunt him down to kill him, but seriously, it's beautiful. I haven't ever seen myself look so good. That's not a hardship."

"I get it, it just seems like you should have gotten something out of that. I'm sure he made a pretty penny off of that picture."

"I've got money, April, and that's not going to buy what I want, which is my heart back. So a check from him is meaningless to me."

"I get it. I just hate that you got taken advantage of. You deserve better than you've gotten with the men in your life."

"Thanks, I agree, but that's the way it goes. I'm just trying to move on from both Matt and Garrett. It will just take time.

We pull in the driveway at Matt's parents' house at about seven-thirty p.m. and both cars are home, plus Steve's truck, and Tara's Honda. The only one missing is Johnny. I've missed all of them, but I'm a little nervous, too. There's no instruction book on how you proceed with your dead, cheating husband's family after the fact. I've loved them all a long time so I try to focus on that as I ring the doorbell with my sister at my side.

Chapter Eight
Lisa

We are passed around for hugs and hellos and led to the family room. As we enter I happen to glance at the mantle and notice there are two, new framed pictures. Taking tentative steps, I walk over and pull the first one down. It's of a sweet, cherub faced little girl with a beautiful, bright smile. She looks happy, and she looks just like Matt. This is without a doubt, Mariah. Crickets aren't even making noise, it is so quiet as everyone watches me with bated breath.

My words are quiet and a little sad as I note, "She has his eyes and his smile. I saw a picture once, right after she was born so I knew about the eyes, but that smile is, just…wow."

I swallow, working to free the lump that's formed in my throat as I fight the tears. I can't imagine how they must feel when they see her. It's crazy how strong the resemblance is.

"I'm sorry, Lisa. I should have taken that down," Judy says, standing beside me now reaching for the photo.

"No, no way, Judy. She's beautiful and she's a part of you. You shouldn't take it down for me. It was just a shock how much she looks like him. She really is cute. How are things going with you guys and Jill and Mariah?"

Judy replies before anyone else can, "They are very good. We get to see her a lot. Jill moved here right after you moved away." She goes on to summarize the sad circumstances Jill and Mariah were living in and it's during this conversation I realize that things may not have been what they seemed when I met her. With minimal education and no family support, Jill was on the verge of being homeless when she contacted me to access Matt's estate. Although the payments are helping, Jill is still having to work two jobs to make ends meet and is having to rely on Matt's family a lot. They don't seem to mind, but for some reason it makes me sad that she's giving up all that time with her baby just to pay the bills.

I clear my throat and place the picture back up on the mantle the way I found it. "I'm serious, I'm okay, guys. This is what I wanted for you all. It would be such a waste for Jill to be alone raising her when she could have this crowd. Don't worry about me. Just be happy you have her."

I smile and wipe the few tears that slipped out and turn my focus to the other picture. It's of me on the beach in Florida. The same picture as the billboard advertisement. Garrett's picture. "How did you get this?" I ask as surprise colors my tone.

"It came in the mail about three weeks ago. It was in a travel magazine and it took just one glance for us to realize it was you. The picture was so fantastic we couldn't help but frame it. Why didn't you tell us you're modeling?" Judy asks.

I fill them in with the PG version of my time with Garrett as Judy pulls out a magazine next to her recliner. The magazine spread includes pictures of my morning run along the beach, one while I'm wading in the water, and one while I'm reading on my lounger with the umbrella.

As I'm studying them John pipes up from his spot and says, "Flip the page, Lisa. There are more."

When I flip the page I see glossy, full-color shots of our day in Crystal River and Three Sisters Springs. I hadn't seen these. I'm floored. I look so damn happy in them that my heart aches a little at the memory.

"Holy crap! He used them all," I breathe out.

This time Tara speaks up, "You really didn't know he was going to use them?"

"No. I had stars in my eyes. I liked the guy a lot and I think it distracted me."

"Oh. Oh." Her eyebrows rise to her hairline, her mouth a perfect O shape.

"He's the guy? I don't know how I knew, but I knew you'd met someone while you were away. What happened?"

I look around knowing I should feel awkward about having this discussion with my dead husband's family, but I think we passed that with the picture of the child he helped conceive while we were still married.

"He wasn't a commitment kind of guy. He was just a man on my vacation that paid me some attention. I haven't spoken to him since before I left Florida on that trip."

"Did you sign a release for the photos?"

"No, to be honest, I thought he used them like a pick up line or a gimmick to get my attention. April asked me the same thing."

My nausea is back full force with all the talk of Garrett so I do my best to steer the conversation toward my life and all the local gossip. It's a nice evening and I'm glad I came.

****

The rest of my weekend passes in a blur with my family and friends. When Sunday morning rolls around, I'm crouched in front of the toilet puking my guts up when I glance at my watch and note that it's time to start packing. I should've done that last night. I drag my exhausted self back into my room to find my mom waiting for me. She's seated on the edge of my bed, her ankle propped up on the opposite knee and her arms crossed over her chest. That stance never means a good conversation is coming.

"Who's the father?" she blurts out.

My eyebrows jump to my hairline as my eyes go wide and muscles string tight. "Wh—Wha—What?"

"I asked...who is the father?" Her voice is quiet but stern. Her body language tells me she's not going anywhere until she gets the truth. "It's obvious you're pregnant. I've been waiting for you to tell me, but you haven't and you're leaving in an hour so you'd better spit it out."

I'm a little bewildered as I answer. "Um... I'm not pregnant. I've just been a little blue since I found out about Matt's baby and made the move to Florida. You know, like I was after he died."

"Oh, my dear. Do you think I just fell off of a turnip truck?"

"What? No!" I squeak out.

"Honey, I've been pregnant, my sisters have been pregnant and your sister has been pregnant. I know it when I see it. You. Are. Pregnant. Now, are you going to tell me who the father is?"

"Oh, God! Do you really think I am?" I plop down on the bed next to her. The weight of the world suddenly heavy on my shoulders.

She gives me 'the look'. I've been getting it since I was a kid.

"Yes. I do. Are you telling me you didn't know?"

"Yes. That's what I'm telling you. I thought I needed to find a counselor in Florida. I planned on doing that once I got back home."

"Now, are you going to fess up?"

"I met a man when I was in Florida on vacation. It was the only time in my life I'd done something like that."

"So, you don't know who he is?" She's looking horrified.

"Yes, of course I know who he is, but he was pretty clear that he was not the commitment kind of guy and I haven't talked to him since."

"Do you know how to contact him?"

"I met his family, so I could probably find him that way, but I don't know if that's such a good idea."

"It's the only idea. Even if he doesn't want anything to do with this baby, you at least need to let him know what's happening. It's the only right thing to do. Finish packing, I'm going to run to the drug store and buy a pregnancy test. No matter what, I'll be here for you. Granted, Ohio is a long way from Florida, but I'll always help you. I'll be back in a few minutes." She places a motherly kiss on top of my head as she stands and leaves the room.

Shit. I went to my gynecologist before I moved to Florida just to make sure I didn't catch any STD's from the stupid unprotected sex I had with Garrett, but it must have been too early to detect pregnancy. When all of that came back clear I didn't think I had any need to go back.

My mom returns from the store and sits with me while I take the test. My nervous hands are shaking as I pick up the test to read the results. Of course, it's positive. I have no idea what I'm going to do and no time to sit with my mom to contemplate it. I have to leave in twenty minutes to catch my flight. I swear my mom to secrecy and promise to call her when I get home. She cries harder when I leave this time than she did when I moved. Now I'm wondering why in the hell I had to move so far away from my family.

I kiss everyone goodbye and head out. On my way through the airport, I have to stop and look at the billboard again. I can't help myself. I still can't believe the person I'm looking at in that picture is me...right before I got knocked up.

Chapter Nine
Lisa

On Monday morning, I call Mark. "Hey, Mark. It's Lisa."

"Hey! Sorry I missed you this weekend. We went up north to see Jessica's grandparents for the holiday."

"I understand. Did you have fun?"

He chuckles before saying, "As much as you can with an eighty-year old couple and their spoiled poodle."

I laugh a little in return and then tell him, "Listen, I want to request a change in the allotment for Jill and Mariah."

"Hmmm...That's going to be difficult because she'll have to sign off on it and I doubt she will do that willingly. Why?" He's not hiding the fact that he's suspicious of this request.

I tell him, "I saw Matt's family while I was in Cincy. Jill moved to Amelia. She's working two jobs and they are helping her as much as they can, but she's missing a lot of time with her kid. It's not Mariah's fault that this whole thing happened like it did. She needs more time with her mother. Jill is being generous, sharing Mariah with Matt's family. A little more help could go a long way. If we increase the monthly to one thousand dollars and allow her to request additional for necessities when they come up, of course you'd have to approve them, it will still leave Mariah with enough for college and plenty for the allotment at twenty-five and thirty-years old. Even if those later numbers are less, I think that it will have the most benefit for Mariah while she's under her mother's care. Matt's family has gotten to know Jill and they think she's a good person and a hard worker. She can still work hard and have some more time for her kid. I don't think she will argue that. Will you do that, please?"

"Are you sure this is what you want?" It's obvious he's skeptical. I'm certain he thinks I've lost it.

I let out the breath I've been holding and answer, "Yeah, I'm done being bitter and judgmental. She's allowing Matt's family to have a relationship with Mariah and it's helping them to heal. She could have been a bitch, but she hasn't been. I want to make it easier on all of them. I think I've finally accepted that Matt screwed Jill over, too. She's not the villain I originally made her out to be and it feels better showing compassion in this situation than it does hatred."

"I'll contact her lawyer and then draw up the paperwork. That's pretty amazing what you're doing for them, Lisa."

"Nah, it's what I should have done in the first place. I'm just glad I figured it out before too much time passed. Just make it a stipulation that Matt's family gets to continue building a relationship with Mariah, please."

"Sure thing."

We hang up and I sit thinking about just how far I've come in a couple months' worth of time. Moving to Florida and gaining some perspective is the best thing I could have done. Now I just have to figure out how to handle things with Garrett. That will not be an easy fix and I'm terrified that he won't want a relationship with his kid. I understand he doesn't want one with me, but I'm praying he'll want one with our child. For the first time since Jill showed up on my doorstep, I have an idea of what she was feeling and it hurts.

Later that afternoon I'm sitting at my desk when Francis, the receptionist, comes to my office with a delivery guy in tow.

"Ms. Browning? I have a package for you and I need your signature."

Francis rolls her eyes and crosses her arms over her chest. "I told him I could sign for it and you'd still get it, but he needs *you* to sign for it."

"That's a specific directive from the sender, ma'am. I'm just doing my job," the delivery guy says, more than a little annoyed.

"That's fine, Francis. No big deal."

I take the package and look for a return label, but don't locate one. I open it to find the same glossy, four-page advertisement about visiting Florida that Matt's parents had. Then I pull out an eight by ten of me sitting on the beach at sunset, the one on the cover of the brochure, minus the writing, framed and beautifully matted. Attached to the back is an envelope. I open it with shaking hands and pull out a handwritten letter and a check. The check has a lot of zeros and is made out to me. I open the letter:

Dearest Lisa,

By now, I'm certain you've seen the ad, but in case you haven't, I included it. When we met I was shooting for the tourist council of Florida and the pictures of you were the ones chosen. I didn't want to share those. They felt personal and private, but they are stunning and the best of my shots by far. The check is your half of the payment for their use. Don't be surprised if people start tracking you down to model for them. I've had a lot of requests for your name. I've refused to share it thus far, hoping to keep the true beauty that is you in my heart.

Leaving you that day was one of the hardest things I've ever done, but I couldn't stay and be one more person who'd hurt you. Seeing your pain, even in those brief moments, gutted me. I hope this finds you happy at your new job. I had to do a little digging to find out where you were. I hope that doesn't sound too creepy.

As for the picture, I wanted you to have a copy of the most stunning photograph I've ever taken. I hope it will remind you of a happy time and of someone who thinks the sun rises and sets with you. Take care of yourself.

Heart & Soul,

Garrett

I get up and close my office door as I feel the tears building. With the hormones running rampant in my system my emotions feel like a pressure cooker just waiting to explode. Anger and hurt swirl inside of me, wounding me further. Just when I think I'm making personal progress with all the loss and dysfunction in my life something reminds me that I'm not quite over him and it all comes back. I'm sure the pregnancy hormones don't help either. What does he mean by *'someone who thinks the sun rises and sets with you'* and signing it *'Heart & Soul'* that's just cruel. It takes me a little bit, but I pull myself back together and finish out my workday.

That night I take a longer than usual jog with Barry at my side while my mind tries to process everything. It was thoughtful that he sent me the check and the pictures, but I could have done without the letter. That's the part that hurts and has me feeling as raw as undercooked meat. I'm wishing he'd never included that. All I can think of now are the moments I shared with him and how warm his skin felt against mine, how demanding he was when he was aroused, the spicy scent of his cologne, and how fantastic he was sexually.

Then I think about the baby and wonder how he's going to react to this news. I'm scared to find him and tell him. I hate feeling scared. It's an emotion too close to helpless for me. I go home angry and frustrated and sadly, wishing he were here.

Chapter Ten
Lisa

On Monday morning Nancy calls me into her office to tell me that we have been invited to the annual United Way Christmas party in Miami. Directors are invited every year and encouraged to go. My first thought is of Garrett. He lives in Miami, but he did say that he's never there. Maybe I should try to track him down while I'm in town and tell him the news. I'm not sure if I'm ready for that though. I haven't told Nancy or anyone other than my family, but I guess if I'm going to try to take a detour while I'm there I'd better explain why.

****

Two weeks later, Nancy and I are clicking on our high heels into the lobby of the Ritz Carlton South Beach. I'm in a knee length, fitted, sleeveless, black dress. Thank goodness I'm not showing much and Nancy is in a red, strapless, floor-length dress. This is the nicest lobby I've ever been in so I can't imagine what the dining room will be like. The weather is beautiful despite the fact that it's mid-December so we spent a couple of hours on the beach today. It left me with some color and Nancy's naturally dark skin with an extra glow.

As we near the dining room, I excuse myself and find the ladies room. When I'm done I freshen up my lipstick and head back out. As I'm turning the corner my eyes are drawn to the most captivating woman I've ever seen. She has to be a movie star, or model, or something. She's wearing a navy gown with crystal beading covering the entire dress and a slit almost all the way up to her hip. She's tall, taller than me, and lean with bronze skin and silky brown hair that is all pulled around to the front over her right shoulder. Her full lips are painted with a shiny, sexy red lipstick and her teeth are perfect, straight and white.

I realize I may have been staring too long when her eyes turn to meet mine. I blush a little, embarrassed to be caught, give a small smile and turn to go. That's when I realize that I'm going the wrong direction.

Damn. Now I have to turn around and walk past the woman in the dress that I was just staring at to get to the dining room. I do my best to avoid eye contact and hustle past her. Being as coordinated as a baby giraffe in my new four-inch heels I stumble and catch myself, but drop my clutch to the floor. It pops open, my lipstick rolls away, my cell phone hits the floor with a thud, and my credit card falls out. I bend down to pick it all up, glancing around pleased that no one noticed. When I stand, I realize the woman's date is now in front her and they are both in profile. My eyes trail up the body of a man I'd know anywhere as I stifle a gasp. Unbelievable. It's Garrett.

The whole world stops for me. I can't breathe. I can't think. It's like I'm frozen in time.

He's dressed in a black tuxedo that screams pure sin the way it compliments his broad shoulders, narrow hips and long muscular legs. It has to be tailored to fit. His hair is shorter than the last time I saw him. His skin is still brown from the sun and his smile also the same, heart stopping. He's standing with his hand on the stunner's waist, very close. She's watching his mouth as he talks to her through a smile it's clear he can't hold back and I'm caught in a weird place. I want to run so he won't see me but I also want to march right up and slap that handsome face of his.

I'm lucky they are so into each other that the distraction of my purse hitting the floor didn't draw their attention. I don't think I could handle seeing his reaction to me as he stands at her side. It's pathetic that I've been pining over him. I was so sad over the last couple of months that I didn't want to get out of bed at times. And I'm pregnant with his child, tired, achy and nauseous while he's dating a beautiful model woman who makes him smile like he just won the lottery. I feel stupid and angry and heartsick. No wonder he didn't want to make a commitment to me, he has women like this to go out with. Ugh. My stomach rolls over at the thought.

I'm not sure how much time passes, but it finally occurs to me that I'm a dumbass watching it all play out with Garrett who is now a millimeter from kissing the goddess in the dress. I turn as fast as I can and hurry toward the ballroom where dinner is being held. I locate Nancy at a table in the back. Her happy smile disappears, replaced with concern the second she sees me. I can't imagine what my face looks like and I can't seem to find a good fake smile to plaster on. Seeing Garrett in this hotel with that woman has me in an emotional tailspin. I'm not sure I'd be more shocked if Matt showed up from the grave right now.

Nancy asks if I'm okay so I nod and tell her we

will talk later. I can't talk about it now. I'll break into a thousand little pieces if I have to go there now. I had explained the basics to Nancy earlier and planned to find Garrett tomorrow before we leave town, but I don't think I can do it now. If I knock on the door and that beautiful woman answers I'll lose it right there on his doorstep. I know I'll come unglued like I never have before.

I miss the keynote speaker and all of the information that's shared with us. I'm too busy chastising myself in my head, wondering why I care that he's with the most beautiful woman in the world instead of me. I slept with the man a few times and spent less than a week with him. This shouldn't be an issue.

Except that it is.

We should be able to share parenthood of this baby without emotions getting in the way. I'm going to have to figure out how to deal with him dating other people or even one someone else before I can face him with this.

That night sleep eludes me. I spend half the night being heartbroken and half the night being pissed that the heartbreaker has moved on to beautiful, sexier things. I know he's not mine, never really was, but the jealousy that's burning its way through my veins is threatening to consume me. By the time I get my wake up call, I'm a hot mess. I shower, throw clothes on, and head for the lobby to find Nancy.

She takes one look at me and says, "I wasn't going to mess with you last night, but coming down here looking like that…" She looks me up and down like I'm missing a screw. "Means you don't get that same luxury on the ride home. Time to start talking, girl."

I explain that I won't be finding Garrett while we are in town. Once we get on the road I fill her in. I know I shouldn't be telling my boss any of this, but I haven't really made any friends since I've moved to Florida and to be honest I need to talk.

At the end of my story she says, "I saw her when she came off the elevator. I can't even imagine how you must feel. I think I've seen her somewhere. Maybe she's a model or something."

"Maybe. It doesn't really matter what she is, what matters is that she was with the man that I'm not quite over, my baby-daddy, and he looked happy. I'm not happy. That week with him was the only true happiness I've known in almost a year and a half. My husband died and I found out not long after his death that he was a big, fat, cheater. Found out that he got a girl pregnant and that she wasn't the only one he was sleeping with. I'm glad that Garrett can move right along, but I'm not having that same experience. I'm still hurting and I'm freaking pregnant to top it off! I wish I'd never met the bastard. Hot beach sex isn't worth all of this."

"The beach sex was that hot?" she asks with a curious look on her face.

"Um...Yeah, yeah, it was. And that makes me madder! Other than leaving me at his parents' house without a proper goodbye he was freaking perfect."

"I don't know what to say, Lisa."

"Nothing you can say. I'm sorry I unleashed all of this on you. That was TMI, I'm sure."

"It's okay, honey. Sometimes talking to someone helps."

I don't say anything else the whole way home. I

pick up Barry from the kennel and take an extra-long run that afternoon trying to burn off stress and excess emotion.

I go into a kind of numb mode over the next week, not leaving the house for anything except work and running. By Saturday, it becomes clear that I have to shop for Christmas presents and mail them by Monday or they won't make it to Ohio in time so I head to the mall.

The mall is crowded and people are ruder than usual. In years past I had most of my shopping done by this point, but this year I just haven't felt up to it. Now I'm paying the consequences. My feet are aching, and I'm starving, but the baby section in Macy's has caught my eye and I'm not paying attention to anything but the tiny little onesie on the hanger in front of me. I'm standing there with all of my bags over one arm and my free hand covering my stomach for a long time. I'm barely showing, but I'm always drawn to placing my hand over that area when I think about the baby. When I turn to leave I bump right into a sturdy male chest. I tilt my head up to apologize and realize I'm staring right at Tommy, Garrett's brother.

His eyes register concern. "Lisa, are you okay?"

"I…I…I…yes. Yes, I'm fine. How are you?" I paint on a fake smile and square my shoulders as I finish.

To his left and back a step or two is a Barbie doll-looking blonde who is giving me the evil eye. Her ample cleavage is on show and she's puffing out her chest like I should be concerned.

I put my hand out, "Hi, I'm Lisa, I'm a friend of Tommy's brother."

She seems to relax a little, but still eyes me curiously when she slides her palm to mine in a wet-fish-handshake, "I'm Mitzi."

Of course she is.

Then she wraps her free arm around his and squishes her breasts to his forearm. Oh geez. I'm not in the mood for this crap. No need to mark your territory lady. He's not the brother I want.

"It was good to see you, Tommy, but I should go."

"Are you pregnant?" he blurts out.

"What? Why would you ask me that?" I feign innocence.

"Because you're standing in the baby section holding your stomach like there might be something inside. Are you pregnant, Lisa?"

Silence stretches uncomfortably between us until I finally nod. "Yes. Just a few months."

I try to keep from elaborating. I don't want to lie to him, but I also don't think I should tell him before I tell his brother.

"Oh shit. It's Garrett's isn't it?"

I guess I misjudged his perceptiveness. I don't say a word.

"Have you told him?"

I just blink up at him. Why am I having this conversation in the middle of Macy's again?

He shakes away from Mitzi as he grabs my arm and pulls me into the deserted baby section and holds one finger up to an impatient Mitzi while he says to her, "Give me a few minutes, babe. I'll find you. Why don't you go find a dress for our date tonight? My treat."

This seems to make her happy so she blows him a kiss and teeters away on her sky-high heels to the ladies section.

"Lisa? What in the hell is going on? Have you told my brother?"

Shaking my head with tears welling up in my eyes, I answer, "No, I haven't. I was in Miami a week ago and was going to find him and tell him, but I saw him at a hotel with a gorgeous model and he looked too happy to interrupt with this kind of news. A girlfriend was too much of a commitment, what do you think he's going to do or say about a baby?"

Tommy runs both hands through his hair and links them at the back of his head. His eyes lift to the ceiling. Clearly exasperated, he cusses under his breath while I fidget and roll my lips between my teeth.

"Fuck, Lisa. Do you plan to tell him? You shouldn't keep this from him. That's not cool." His hands fall to his sides and he places them on his hips. I don't reply. "Do you plan to keep it?"

"I plan to tell him, but I'm not expecting anything from him. I don't have his number so I couldn't call. Yes, I plan to keep it. That was never a question for me."

"Goddamn, this is a mess. Are you okay? Do you need anything? You obviously got the job in Orlando. Are you happy?" His questions come at me rapid fire and it takes me a second to respond.

"Yeah, it's a really big mess. I'm in a new town with no support system. I'm considering moving back to Cincy before the baby is born. I just don't know what to do. I'm feeling a little shell-shocked to be honest. I have my first doctor appointment on Tuesday, but I assume everything is okay. I appreciate you asking, but no, I don't need anything. Well, I probably do need

Garrett's number. I deleted it after he left me at your parent's house. Thought I'd never need it again."

Putting his hand out in front of him he says, "Give me your phone, Lisa."

I hand it over to him and he starts typing. "I'm adding my number, Garrett's number, and my parent's numbers. If you need anything, ever, please call us. I'm calling my phone now so I have your number. I'll be checking on you. I'm not real excited to leave you without knowing you're taken care of. This is crazy."

"Tell me about it. I've been on birth control for years. I can't believe it failed me this time. I promise to call you if I need anything. Please don't tell him. Let *me* tell him. This kind of information needs to come from me. I'd like to do it after the New Year. The holidays are hard enough being alone. I don't think I'd take it well if his response isn't favorable."

"Alright, I'll give you time to do it your way, but promise me you will tell him. I can't guarantee how he'll react, but he'd want to know. I'm sorry I didn't say goodbye to you that weekend. I didn't realize my brother was gonna be a dick and ruin it for all of us. Just so you know, we all think he's an idiot. My parents loved you and I like you a lot, too. You were good for him." His smile is soft and sincere so I know he means it.

I avert my eyes to the floor and shake my head as the sadness consumes me once again. "Well he's moved on just fine now, it's not a big deal. I feel bad that he'll have the reminder of that week forever, but I don't regret it. I'm just glad I met all of you. You probably need to go find your girlfriend before she buys the whole store. It was good to see you."

He hugs me tight and I almost cry.

"No matter what my brother decides, the rest of us will want you and the baby in our lives so keep that in mind. Okay?"

"Okay, I'll be sure to stay in touch."

He gives my cheek a gentle pat and strides away.

Garrett

Well, it's official. I'm a pussy. I must have left my man-card in Lisa's purse when I took off that morning because I haven't seen even an ounce of my manhood since I was in her bed. It's not like I haven't had opportunity. There is always plenty of that, especially in New York City, but I couldn't bring myself to seal the deal with any of the prospects. Couldn't even leave the bar with them. Then the worst one of all was Lana. She's the reason I *know* I'm missing my man-card. She called and asked me to attend a charity gala in Miami with her a couple of days before I left for Europe and I agreed thinking that I would finally end this drought.

It's arguable that she's one of the sexiest women in the world. We've been together before and it was pretty hot so I thought it would be a sure thing this time. However, Lana *freaking* Payton, international supermodel, stood right in front of me begging me to stay with her, begging me to screw her and I couldn't pull the trigger. Truth be told, the stunner didn't do a single thing for me. All I could do was catalogue all the things about her that weren't like Lisa.

Now I'm sitting by the fire at this posh ski lodge in the Swiss Alps, with a glass of whiskey in one hand and a picture of Lisa in the other, wishing I'd have done things differently.

My colleagues left a few hours ago to head to a

nightclub. I declined to join them. When they pressed me about why I wasn't going I lied and said I had work to catch up on. I've worked with most of these people before so they know I'm full of shit. They just don't know why. I've been short tempered since I got here which is also unlike me. If I were sleeping better at night and drinking a little less my mood might improve, but I don't see that in my near future.

My mom's words to me the morning I left Lisa seem to roll around my head like marbles in a jar. Her words are on repeat, making things worse, *Rhett, she's the one. I know it, you know it, we all know it. Don't make the mistake of a lifetime and let her go. You'll be sorry. I know you will. Please listen to me for once, son.*

As I stare out the window to the dark night beyond the lodge, my phone buzzes on the table alerting me to a text from my brother. I pick it up and read: *Hey, man. You need to call me ASAP.*

My mind instantly jumps to my parents, worried that something has happened, so my fingers fly over the number as quick as possible.

"That was fast." By the tone of his voice I can picture the smirk on his face.

"You said ASAP." If he's messing with me, I'll be pissed.

"Yeah, well I wanted to make sure you called me. That hasn't been your strong suit the last few months and it's important." Now he sounds a little testy.

"Are Mom and Dad okay?" I question.

"Mom and Dad are fine. So are Jackie, Jase, and Olivia. It's not that."

"Well, what is it that's so important you had to freak me out?" I allow him to hear the irritation I'm feeling.

He sighs and then says, "I ran into Lisa at the mall in Orlando a few days ago."

My heart stops. Did he just say Lisa? A sliver of fear swirls around my neck, choking me a little. "Um…Is she okay?" I'm sure the worry is evident in my voice. I'm trying not to give away the desperation I feel for information about her.

"Yeah, she is, but you need to talk to her." He sounds a little more bossy than usual.

"Why? What's going on?" I stand up to pace as we talk. My heart is racing at the mention of her name and my stomach is clenching and unclenching like someone has a fist around it.

"You just need to talk to her. Call her. I have her number if you want it. I'm trying to get her to come to Mom and Dad's Christmas party."

"Why, man? That's not cool. I'm not seeing her anymore." If this is some crazy attempt to get us back together I'll be pissed.

"Yeah, I hear ya. You're full of shit. How many times have you been laid since you dumped her at Mom and Dad's?"

"Why is that your business?" I sit down on the edge of the couch and run my left hand across my short hair in agitation.

"Just answer the damn question."

He knows he's hit the mark. I let silence fill the air, not wanting to say the answer out loud.

"That's what I thought. Call her you dumb ass. You know you want too and I know she'd want to hear from you. Even if you don't want her back you have to promise to call her, okay? For me? It's very important."

"Okay, yes. I can do that. I'll call her when I get home after the New Year, but do you have to invite her for the Christmas party? I don't want to hurt her by giving her false hope."

A deep sigh fills my ear before he says, "Yes, man. She's alone for Christmas. She's not going back home and she doesn't have any friends here yet. She knows you don't want anything to do with her. She even said so when I ran into her. All I ask is that you call her. Sooner, rather than later. I love you, bro. Merry Christmas."

"Love you, too. Merry Christmas."

A few hours go by and I'm in worse shape than before. My brother did a Jedi mind-fuck on me by calling with that request.

In the middle of the night, I give up the fight, unable to sleep, I make a decision that I'm certain is what my brother was hoping for. I could kick his ass. In fact, I may just do that when I get home. I'm leaving the day after tomorrow and hoping to arrive in Orlando on Christmas day.

I called my travel agent to change my flight and get a rental car. I'm tired of trying to ignore this. My dumb ass fell in love and no matter how much I'd like to deny it, I can't anymore. My brother's phone call just solidified it. It's time to fight for the girl. The question is, will she still want me after how I treated her?

Lisa

A week after my shopping trip, I get a call from Tommy. I debate about not picking it up, but then I decide I might as well get it over with. He said he'd be checking on me so I'd better answer.

"Hello?" I try for a cheerful tone.

"Hey, Lisa. It's me, Tommy."

"Yeah, I know. I have caller ID, remember?" I giggle.

"Oh, yeah. You busy?"

"Sort of. What's up?"

"My mom made me call. My parents have a huge Christmas party every year. This one is on Christmas Eve. It starts at six p.m. You can crash at their place so you don't have to drive home if you want. It's a potluck thing out at my uncle's property in the woods. There are tons of people there and it's a lot of fun. They want you to come if you aren't leaving town for Christmas."

"I'm not, but I don't think that's a good idea. Garrett would be upset if I showed."

"It's a great idea. Besides, Garrett is not coming home this year. He left last week on assignment to the Swiss Alps. He won't be home until January 3rd. Come on. I'm sure you don't have anything better to do. You can even bring that dog of yours. He did come with you to Florida, right?"

"Yeah, Barry came with me. I don't know. Let me think about it, okay?"

"Okay, but we're all hoping you'll come." His voice is sweet, his words genuine.

"Thanks, Tommy. I have to get going, please say hello to your parents for me."

"Take care, Lisa. Hope to see you soon. Let me know."

I take the next couple of days to decide, but in the end I decline. I know it's a bad idea, building a relationship with his family behind his back. He needs to decide how much contact he wants with the baby and then we can discuss what to do about his family. He needs to know first and since he's out of the country until the New Year I can't talk to him yet.

I send a text declining the visit, but thanking him for the invite. I call a florist in Crystal River and request that a ginormous Christmas bouquet be sent to their home. I luck out because the florist is actually going to the party and said she'd deliver it then. Gotta love a small town. I ask the florist to attach a note that reads: *Sorry I couldn't make it. Hope you all have a Merry Christmas! Love, Lisa Browning*

Then I go to the store and buy, a small turkey breast, stuffing, green beans, and apple pie to make myself the next day. I figure I could share some with Barry if it's way too much.

I go to bed that night and cry myself to sleep, wondering what I was thinking to move so far from home and then not go back for Christmas. The word lonely doesn't even begin to describe how I feel. I've spent the days since I saw Tommy looking at baby stuff online. That has kept me busy, but I'm still so lonesome. Probably more than I was my first Christmas without Matt. I cry so hard that Barry rests his face on the side of the bed watching me most of the night.

Chapter Eleven
Lisa

Christmas morning, I watch the parades on television for a little while and then take Barry for a run. We usually walk in the morning, but today I opt for something different so that I don't sit and dwell on the fact that I'm alone. The streets of Orlando are deserted when I start. By the end of my run though, there are families down by the park helping little kids on brand new bikes and kids in their driveways bouncing balls or chasing each other. I smile as I think of the future and the fact that I will be doing the same thing with my child in a few years' time.

As I round the corner to my house I notice someone sitting on my porch steps, head down, elbows on knees, with a suitcase parked next to the front door. He's wearing blue jeans, a red polo shirt, and brown cowboy boots. He lifts his head at the sound of my tennis shoes hitting the pavement and I stop dead in my tracks as my smile collapses. Barry doesn't anticipate the unexpected stop and gets jerked back by the leash when he keeps going.

It's Garrett. You could have knocked me over with a feather.

Barry is pulling on the leash, but I'm stuck in the cement of my own shock. Excited about company on our porch, Barry keeps pulling until the force propels me forward. It's a good thing I don't think of him as my guard dog. The only thing he'd do to an intruder is lick them to death.

"Lisa." My name comes out pained, like it's a struggle.

"Garrett? What are you doing here?" My tone is questioning and a little bit hostile. It's possible I'm not quite over seeing him with the supermodel woman in Miami.

"I had to see you. My brother called after he saw you at the mall and said it was important that I call you. He wouldn't say why. I was having a hard time getting you out of my head anyway so I figured it was a sign."

I move up to the porch and sit on the step near him, just not too close. I'm cursing myself for making that morning run. I'm sweaty, sticky, smelly, and in my freaking workout clothes. A woman never wants to see her ex while she looks like this. That's even more important if he's used to seeing models in bikinis and ball gowns. I'm not showing enough for anyone to guess that I'm pregnant, but I am filling out more than before. My boobs are fuller, as are my hips. My running clothes give that away.

I don't respond to his comment, instead I ask, "How did you find me?"

"Internet web search. Took a little bit, but I got it. If I couldn't find it I was going to get the phone number from Tommy."

I'm not sure what to say to that so I stand up and walk to the door.

"I need a shower. You can come in if you want."

I offer him a drink. He declines and I head for the shower.

The whole time I'm in the shower I try to understand why he's at my house when I know he's been with that woman in Miami and he is supposed to be in the Swiss Alps through the New Year. Once I get done, I put some product in my hair and get dressed. Then I head back out there to face him.

Barry, the big traitor, is laying across the couch with his head in Garrett's lap while his coat is stroked, his eyes closed, tongue hanging out. His tail has a slight wag as he falls deeper into doggie bliss. He's the poster puppy for happiness.

I sit down in the recliner next to the couch and survey the situation. The man who broke my heart is sitting on my couch looking a little disheveled, a lot tired, but content to be rubbing my dog's head.

"Why are you here, Garrett?" Irritation and sadness coat my words.

"I was having a hard enough time without you and then Tommy called saying he saw you. I couldn't stand it. I had to come back. I had to see you."

"Garrett, I can take a lot of things, but lying isn't one of them. Don't you think I got enough of that with my husband?"

"What are you talking about? Of course, I'm telling the truth. I've been a mess since the morning I left you in Crystal River."

"You're lying Garrett." I'm losing control of my anger as I growl out the words. I'm sure my face is red and if someone checked my blood pressure it would now be through the roof.

"Why would you say that? I don't understand." It's obvious he's confused.

I lean forward with my elbows on my knees never

breaking eye contact. "Because I saw you, Garrett. I saw you. In Miami. If you missed me you wouldn't have been with someone else," I grind out through clenched teeth.

"What are you talking about?"

"Beautiful, brunette, long navy and silver evening gown. You, in a tux. The Ritz Carlton, Miami Beach. Any of that ring a bell?" My voice is dripping with sarcasm.

In an instant his face pales and he looks down at the floor. "If you were there, why didn't you say anything?"

"I was less than five feet from you and you were so damn preoccupied with her that you didn't notice me. *Less. Than. Five. Feet.* Do I look stupid enough to break up that little romantic encounter?" The tears are building as my vision blurs, my nose is burning, and my heart is racing. My hormones are out of control and swinging like monkeys on vines.

"Shit." He shakes his head. He can't meet my eyes he just looks at the floor.

"Why are you really here, Garrett? Don't you think you did enough damage when you left me at your parents' house without a goodbye?" A tear slips down my face and I wipe it away, hoping he doesn't see it.

"I only saw the woman from the Ritz, Lana, once since I saw you in September. That was the night you saw me. She was a model on one of my shoots a few years ago. I've seen her from time to time over the years so I thought it would be okay. I was lonely and she needed a date to a charity gala. I'm sorry you had to see that. I didn't sleep with her though. I couldn't. I got all the way to her room and knew it was wrong, so I left."

"Why. Are. You. Here?" I yell as I jump up out of my chair. I'm losing my cool fast. Barry raises his head away from Garrett to look at me.

Garrett stands and crosses the room, grabbing my shoulders, stepping into my space, panic etched onto his face. "I'm here because I love you. I've never loved a woman in my life besides my mother and sister until you. I wasn't even certain that's what it was. Even kissing Lana felt wrong. I'm serious. I love you, Lisa. I'm sorry for running away from you, for leaving without saying goodbye. I panicked."

He takes a deep breath and quietly says, "I'm all in with you. I screwed up. I know I did, but I'm serious. I want to be with you. I called and cancelled my lease in Miami. I have a company packing my stuff up after the holidays and I'm moving here, to Orlando. I want you back. I want you to be with me, always. I love you. I know I don't deserve you, but I'm praying you'll still give me chance."

"Who else have you been with since you were with me?" Jealousy is still simmering below the surface as I picture him with Lana. My face feels hot and my hands clenched in anger are shaking so much I'm sure he will soon notice.

"No one, I swear. I couldn't do it. You're under my skin. Somehow in less than a week you became a part of my soul. I need you, Lisa. I'm just praying I'm not too late. Are you with someone else?" His eyes are pained and pleading.

I can feel my strength crumbling. The tears I've been holding back start to fall. He steps even closer so our bodies touch, his lips hover over mine. His breath is soft and warm on my face. His cologne, spicy in my nose.

"Don't cry, sweetheart. I'm sorry for everything. I love you. Please give me another chance," he pleads.

I look up into his imploring emerald eyes and this time he whispers, "I love you. I want you. I need you. Only you, always."

I close the distance between us and throw my arms around his neck. So much for being tough. I lasted all of about ten minutes before I crumbled. Passion that's been dormant for months flares to life in an instant and I find myself trying to climb him like a tree. Barry gets the hint and scrambles out of the room to hide in one of the other rooms.

Our lips are fierce and hungry, feasting off of each other. His hands drop to my behind and squeeze the flesh there. A whimper escapes my throat as he turns and pushes my back against the wall, grinding his hips into mine. His lips are hot and wet as they suck on my earlobe and the sensitive spot right behind my ear. God, I love when he hits that spot.

I grind and roll my hips as I direct him, "Straight down the hall, last door on the right. Go!"

He doesn't hesitate. He sucks the skin at the base of my throat hard, leaving a mark I'm certain. Then he grips my backside harder, and carries me down the hall, depositing me on the bed with a thump. I scuttle back to the middle and he crawls across, on top of me. He tugs my shirt over my head and unclasps my bra tossing it across the room. With one fast yank, he pulls my yoga pants and panties off and settles his head between my legs. He kisses the soft, velvety skin of my inner thighs as I wiggle with impatience, praying he will quickly get to where I need him the most. I squirm and pant in desperation.

"Hush, just watch me," he grumbles. I can tell he's changing the pace from fast and eager to slow and easy. My heart continues to gallop at a clipped pace as I prop myself up on my elbows and watch as he swipes at my sleek center with his skilled tongue, his goatee abrading the sensitive skin as he moves. He's hitting every spot along my crease except the one I need. The little bundle of nerves he's avoiding is pulsing and my thighs are shaking with the unreleased tension. It feels like forever since we were last together. His breath is warm and the sound of his enjoyment as he feasts on me has me standing at the edge of a canyon ready for the free fall.

I'd heard once, that pain can bring pleasure and I never understood it until he nips my clit lightly with his teeth. Instant pain is replaced just as fast by waves of consuming pleasure as I come apart at the seams, thrashing and crying out. I don't think I've ever come that quickly before. My whole body bucks with the tremors of my release and my breath comes out choppy and heavy like I just finished a marathon.

He slides back off of the bed and strips off his clothing. I'm eagerly perusing his muscled thighs and long, thick cock, when his shirt goes sailing past my head landing near my nightstand. God I've missed that chest, those abs, and his sexy, broad shoulders

Before he moves back over me, he devours my naked body from head to toe with his eyes and says in a husky voice, "My God, I didn't know it was possible for you to be more beautiful than before. You've put on a little weight and you look so damn good. Every curve sexier than the last time I saw you and I swear your breasts are fuller, more round. Sexy. As. Fuck. Spread your legs, sweetheart."

I panic a little realizing I haven't told him about the baby yet, but he steals my thoughts when he growls out, "Damn, I love this body."

My mind now laser focused on him wills my thighs to part so he can slide between them. His hips roll against mine and he enters me slowly, his motion graceful, every muscle flexing with the movement. He never takes his eyes off mine and the thoughts and panic I had only a second ago are thrust away by the magic of love and pheromones.

Silence in the house is pushed aside by our heavy breathing and passionate moans as we mate. Our bodies unite, sweat slicked and overheated. He lowers his mouth to my sensitive breast taking the berried tip into his mouth with a gentle suck while flicking his tongue. My back arches and I clench him from within. A wicked grin spreads on his handsome face removing the serious expression of a moment ago. His eyes continue to watch me as he moves to the other one repeating the process with more hunger than the first time. I can't keep eye contact, the pleasure he's giving is too great. I squeeze my eyes shut and moan as my back bows again. His mouth releases and his teeth close gently around the beaded nipple. Our hips never stop moving in perfect synchronicity like we've been doing this for years.

"I love you," he whispers right before he rolls to his back taking me with him so I'm on top. I rock my hips building our rhythm again. His hands come up to join with mine and I use them for leverage as I lift higher to come down harder. There is a sweet familiar ache growing in my core. If his thumb touches my clit or I roll my body just right I will detonate with the force of a thousand bombs, but I'm not ready. I love this feeling. The anticipation, the sensual burning that spreads slow like molasses through every muscle and then quick as a whip releases a pleasure so amazing you stop breathing for seconds at a time.

With our hands linked he straightens them over his head, pulling my body down, bringing my lips to his. Our tongues dance together with sensual twists and flicks. I catch his bottom lip between my teeth with a playful nip and then thrust my tongue back inside searching for his. He groans, releases our hands and flips us again. This time he yanks my hips onto his bent knees, bends over me and wraps his arms around my shoulders while he hammers into me harder than I've ever had before, the strength of his hips unmatched.

He's holding me in place to assure that I take everything he has to give. I'm moaning and whimpering as the sweet sensation spreads further, just waiting for the split second when my body lets go. The sound of our skin slapping, groans, grunts and whimpers of passion reverberate off the walls of my room. I'm lost in Garrett and I never want to be found. As I feel our souls connect I close my eyes and hold on tight as our bodies explode together. Nothing else exists in this moment except Garrett and me.

The feel of his sweat covered skin and his muscled weight on mine, the sound of his breath next to my ear as it settles, and the musky smell of sex that covers us both has me living in a moment of beautiful euphoria. He doesn't pull out of me, doesn't move off of me. He just stays with me, inside of me, and there is no place

I'd rather him be.

I whisper, "I love you, too, Garrett. I knew it when we were sitting on your parent's couch watching television that night. I probably even knew it before we left to go to Crystal River."

He moves his face from my neck and places a tender kiss to my lips.

I continue, "I'm scared though. How do I trust there will be no more Lana's? Matt spent a lot of years cheating on me while he traveled and I never knew. I trusted him. I can't go back to being that naive. I can't go back to being that weak, overly trusting person again. And after seeing the way you looked at Lana it will always sit in the back of my mind. That smile you gave her crushed me."

He places his hands on both sides of my head, holding it in place. His eyes burn a hole right through me as he says, "Look at me, sweetheart. Lana means nothing. Turns out she's nothing more than an old friend, more of an acquaintance if I'm being honest. I knew when I left you in Crystal River that I couldn't be who you needed me to be. If I had any doubt about my commitment to you now, I'd never have come here today. I know what you've been through. I held you when you cried after you got confirmation of his baby. I'd never do anything to put you in that position again. I will do everything I can to make sure you know what I'm doing and whom I'm doing it with when I'm off working in a different location. I promise. If the day comes that I can't be faithful anymore I'll end it before I cheat on you. But, I have to be honest; I just can't see that happening, ever. I couldn't even do it when we weren't together. It just felt wrong. I was serious when I said I haven't been with anyone else."

"There will always be a Lana that wants you. How you turned her down I don't know. She's the most beautiful woman I've ever seen. It will be hard when they make it easy for you to have them."

"She might be the most beautiful woman you've ever seen, but *you* are the most beautiful woman *I've* ever seen. She doesn't hold a candle to you. You'll have to learn to trust me, but I will do all I can to make that trust come easy. I thought about it all the way here. I won't take any more assignments out of the country unless it's somewhere you want to go and you can take vacation to go with me. I'll try to take local assignments or ones that only require a minimum amount of time away, like a couple of days. I'll do whatever you need or want me to do to make this work. I cannot live without you."

"I don't want to ruin your career because I'm insecure. That's not fair," I tell him.

"I have enough money to last a very long time. I've taken jobs all over the world for the last ten years, all expenses paid. I had an apartment in Miami, a truck that was paid off a few years ago and no other expenses. I can afford to cut back for a long time. As for ruining my career? That's not going to happen. As long as I continue to produce with the jobs I do accept, it will be okay. But even if it didn't work out I could always open a studio here in town and not travel at all."

"I'd never ask you to do that."

"You don't have to, you are worth it."

"Garrett, there is something you need to know. I don't know how you're going to take it. I was planning on finding you when you got back from Europe." I take a deep breath and let it out, terrified he will run. I want to move out from underneath him. Scoot away and cover up before I utter words that will forever change things. So far this has been too good to be true, more than I ever expected from him.

He must sense that this is going to be a doozy because he rolls off to my side and props his head in his hand. His smoldering green eyes watching me intently.

Then he adjusts the covers up over us, drapes an arm over my hip and says, "Okay, go for it. Whatever it is, just tell me." He appears to be calm, not worried in the least about the news I'm about to share.

The nervousness I'm feeling inside must show on my face because his brow furrows with concern. "Did you find someone else?"

"Well, not really. Not in the sense that you're thinking." Another deep breath in, long exhale. I clench my eyes closed and then I blurt out, "I'm pregnant, Garrett. You're going to be a dad."

My eyes open and I wait for his reaction. There is no sound from him. Not an intake of breath, not a word. Nothing. His eyes are locked on mine, but all expression is wiped away.

"Garrett, I'm sorry. I didn't mean for it to happen. I've been on birth control for years and have never even had a scare. I promise I didn't plan this." It's almost as if I'm pleading for him to understand. Tears line my eyes, ready to spill any second. My anxiety bumping up higher and higher as the silence stretches out.

He drops to his back and runs his fingers over his scalp. Back and forth, back and forth. Stopping with the heels of his hands over his eyes he exhales, but still no words come out. He lays like this for a few minutes.

I'm frightened he's about to bolt so I don't move a muscle, I just cautiously watch him process this information.

It's odd but his first question is, "Does Tommy know?"

"Yes, he caught me in the baby section at Macy's. He knew right away. He was pissed I hadn't told you yet. I'd only known three weeks at that point. I'd been planning to find you when I was in Miami, but when I saw you with Lana I knew I couldn't handle it if she answered your door in the morning. It would have killed me. I planned to contact you after the New Year when you got back."

"I can't believe he didn't tell me."

"I'm sure he wanted to, but I begged him to let me tell you. I felt like the information should come from me. I hadn't even seen the doctor yet when I saw Tommy that day."

"Damn, that's a pretty big piece of information. Give me a little bit to absorb it, okay?"

I scoot away, seeking escape. I don't know if I can wait for him to decide if this is good or bad news. Ten minutes ago, I had everything I've ever wanted and now I'm not so sure that's how this will play out. He reaches out and grabs my arm before I get to the edge of the bed.

"I didn't say I wanted to absorb alone. Come here. It's been too long since I've held you."

Wait. What? Did he really just say that?

As if he's reading my mind he gives my arm a little tug and I allow the tears to roll down my face as I crawl back to him. I lay my head on his chest and hike a leg over his. He wraps both arms around me and holds me close. His heart is loud, thumping at a frantic pace in my ear as I snuggle him quietly. I have to lift my head a few times to wipe tears away, but I return to the same position every time.

"We're really going to have a baby?" His voice is deep, but quiet.

"Yeah, my due date is June 21st. Are you mad?"

"No, not at all. Just…shocked, I guess. I never thought I'd be a dad. I know every single inch of your body, probably better than I know my own. I just figured you've been eating more. I should have known." Realization dawns on him and his eyes widen as his panic sets in. "Oh shit, did I hurt you? Did I hurt the baby? I should have been more careful."

"I'm fine. The baby's fine. All the information says that lovemaking is okay. Don't worry."

"I don't know anything about babies or kids. I don't know how good I'll do at being a dad." He's scared and he doesn't need to be.

"Garrett, stop. All you have to do is be here and love us. We can figure out the rest as we go. Are you really staying? Are you sure that's what you want?"

"Yes, I wouldn't leave you now for anything. I love you. I'm fearful and a little excited at the same time, but there is no way I'm leaving you."

I stay quiet a little longer until he asks, "Do you have to work tomorrow?"

"No, Nancy gave us tomorrow off. I'm not due back to the office until Monday. Why?"

"Let's load up Barry and go to my parent's house. I think this is news we should share in person." He searches my eyes waiting for my response.

"You really want to? You're really okay with

this?"

"I'm more than okay, sweetheart. I'm in love with a woman who's going to have my baby. This may be the best Christmas ever."

His movement is sudden as he leaps out of bed and starts tugging on clothes, an excited energy swirling around him. I haven't moved. I'm too stunned by the turn of events to respond so he gives me a gentle poke in the ribs as a ghost of a smile appears on his face.

"Come on, let's go tell everyone."

Before I can even get dressed he places a kiss on me so deep that I almost forget my name and in this moment I know I've just been given everything I've ever wanted, but never had.

About the Author

Tiffani was born in Texas but has lived all over the United States. She currently resides in Florida with her husband, three daughters and her dog. She graduated from the University of Maryland with a degree in social science and spent five years working for Hospice.

When she's not writing or taxiing her children around she enjoys reading and attending concerts. Tiffani is also a crazed fan of the Tampa Bay Lightning, Tampa Bay Rays, and the Chicago Cubs.

~*~

Visit Tiffani at

http://tiffanilynn.com

~*~

To chat with Tiffani Lynn and other Wild Rose Press authors of erotic romance, join us at

www.groups.yahoo.com/group/thewilderroses.

Also Available

The Arrangement

by

Brandy Ayers

https://amzn.com/B01CKN4CFI

The mind is a tricky thing. No one knows that better than Michelle O'Brian due to maladaptive daydreaming, an undiagnosed disorder that makes HER question the line between reality and fantasy. Forced to change careers after her goal of making a mark in the journalism world implodes, she finds herself unable to stop fantasizing about her new boss. And every other man she comes across.

Her uncontrollable daydreams are a problem at work. Not even an orgasm inducing visit to her sexy as hell friend, Russ Seko, can stem the need for her mind to wander. But as it becomes clear that Russ wants more, and her workplace flirting may not be all pretend, things get out of hand. Fast.

Caught between two men, trapped by her ambition, and fooled by her own mind, how can Michelle trust anything in her life when dreams seem so real?

Also Read

Maybe I Do

by

Allie Fisher

https://amzn.com/B01EVJ9IEY

A controlling mother and a high school sweetheart who broke her heart—only two of the reasons thriving lawyer Katherine Boon left her hometown of Isle of Hope, Georgia.

Twenty years later "Kit" must return for a wedding. Her goal? To get her niece married and get back to her comfortable, normal, single life in California. The last thing she expects is a one-night stand that rocks her world or that said rocker is the man she hired to plan the wedding.

Devout bachelor Aiden Spencer might plan weddings, but he has no interest in one of his own...until he does the unthinkable. He falls for one of his clients. With a little help, he sets out to seduce his way into her bed and into her heart.